KNIGHT SWAM

KNIGHT SWAM

A Novel
by
Katya Lezin

ISBN 978-0-557-20384-0

*To Noah and Hannah, who share
my SCRABBLE obsession,*

*To David and Eliza, who tolerate it,
And to my dad, who first taught me the game.*

CHAPTER ONE

"Is that a hickey?" Joe Fletcher asked incredulously, staring at the red mark on Drew's neck.

Drew had tried covering it up with his t-shirt, stretching it up and over the welt, but all he'd succeeded in doing was creating a neck hole big enough to fit Matt Santoni, who looked like he was the middle linebacker of the Providence High School football team even though he was only in 8th grade. Matt swore that he downed a shake of three raw eggs every morning and that was why he was, as he put it, *so rock solid*, but Drew suspected Matt had come out of the womb that way, huge and menacing, even as an infant.

Guys like Matt Santoni probably cut their bullying teeth in the preschool sandbox, tapping into the radar all bullies seem to have and hone for finding the weaklings, the crybabies, and the ones who comprise the other part of the bullying equation. It was guys like Matt Santoni whom Drew's parents should have visualized when deciding, back in the first grade when Drew was average size, maybe even a little taller than most of the kids in his class, that it would be okay to have him skip a grade.

"He's reading at a fourth grade level," Mrs. Roebucker gushed, beaming with pride at her prowess as an educator, even though Drew's giftedness had little to do with her. He had entered kindergarten able to read chapter books, and it wasn't long before he had become the de facto assistant teacher. Being the only kindergartner who could read the worksheets or the directions on the board made kids gravitate (*v*, to move gradually and steadily to or toward somebody or something as if drawn by some force or attraction) to him to ask for help or for clarifications on what they were supposed to do. Drew remembered it vividly, the way the kids looked up to him and deferred to him, because it was the only time he could recall being popular and respected. Pretty sad, he often thought to himself, that my social peak came in *kindergarten*.

Those same traits that propelled him to a leadership role in kindergarten had the opposite effect from that point onwards. Even in second grade, kids saw him as a nerd – in *second* grade! – and he was never able to shake it. Drew came by his nerdiness naturally, having inherited it from both his parents. Looking at them sometimes, huddled over a fierce SCRABBLE game or excitedly opening their monthly issues of National Geographic or The New York Review of Books, Drew realized he was doomed from the start. The thought of his dad throwing a football with him or his mom staying current on the latest fashions was laughably ludicrous (*adj,* utterly ridiculous because of being absurd, incongruous, impractical or unsuitable). His dad didn't follow any sports teams and offered outings to the symphony or the ballet – the ballet, no joke! – as his version of father-son bonding. His mom had no clue who was on TV or at the movies – if it wasn't in the pages of a book, it held zero interest to her.

Mara and Sam Founts-Hiltone were both voracious (*adj,* ravenous) readers. They'd met in a Russian literature class at Brown University and books figured heavily in their courtship. Sam Founts gave Mara Hiltone a copy of <u>Pride and Prejudice</u>, in lieu of flowers, on their first date, and she told her roommate that night that she'd met the man she would marry. She figured a guy who appreciates Jane Austen was a definite keeper. Mara returned the favor with a signed copy of Roald Dahl's memoir, <u>Flying Solo</u>. It was a prized possession, given to her by her grandfather, but she told herself that it was really more of a loan, since it would most likely end up as neither hers nor his but theirs, on a joint bookshelf. And it was only natural that two lovers of literature would read to their child, starting when he was still in Mara's ever-expanding tummy. By the time Drew was ready to tackle books on his own, they all had a familiar ring because he'd read most of their collection of children's books while he was still in the womb.

Mara and Sam even went so far as to give Drew the middle name of Red, which was an intentional double entendre. First, it was pronounced the same way as the past tense of read (*v,* to look at so as to take in the meaning of, as something written or printed), a favorite activity of theirs and one they hoped to cultivate in their little prodigy. Second, it reflected the color of their son's hair, which began as a carrot-hued layer of fuzz and grew into curls the same color that many women spent half a day at the beauty salon trying to emulate (*v,* to try to equal or surpass). So red-headed Drew Red Founts-Hiltone did, in fact, live up to his name, and by the end of kindergarten, he was so far ahead of his peers that Mrs. Roebucker strongly encouraged Sam and Mara to have him skip first grade.

To their credit, Drew's parents did hesitate. They had no doubt Drew was ready academically, but they did worry about how the age gap would play out later, in middle and high school.

"But he'll be bored to death if he doesn't," Mrs. Roebucker insisted.

And this is the point at which Drew claims his parents failed him. They should have stood their ground. So what if he was a little bored? He didn't know any students who *weren't* bored. And if he could have had a say, at least the fast-forwarded version of Drew who was way height-challenged to begin with *and* behind in the puberty race, he'd have picked boredom any day over what he got instead. Because the truth was, he was *still* bored. Academically, school was pretty much a snooze fest. The only excitement in his day stemmed from his almost daily battle to stay alive. His parents should have envisioned Matt Santoni, who could lift Drew up with one hand while simultaneously giving him an atomic wedgie (a feat he'd been willing to demonstrate on more than one occasion) and all the other kids, including the girls, who literally towered over their precious genius child. And they should have known that being gifted in first grade is cause for kudos and pride. Being gifted in middle school, when you haven't yet hit puberty and knowing the number for pi down to 42 digits has zero social cache, is pretty much a death sentence.

"Drew's got a hickey! Drew's got a hickey!" Joe announced to the rest of the bus, an announcement that was met with incredulous whoops and cheers. Guesses as to who the lucky lady was, none of them kind, were yelled out the entire ride home. Drew stared out the window, wishing his stretched-out shirt could hide more than just the supposed hickey, and concentrated mightily on trying not to cry.

"But why," Dr. Anderson asked, when Drew recounted the hickey incident to him at their weekly session, "was this so devastating to you?"

When Drew simply shook his head, refusing to answer, Dr. Anderson tried again.

" You have been teased like this before, but I can see that this time was particularly troubling to you. Can you explain to me why that is?"

Drew stared at Dr. Anderson's fish tank, trying to figure out if a new fish had been added to replace the little spotted one that the large yellow and blue striped fish had eaten, right before Drew's own eyes, during his session two weeks earlier.

"Because," Drew finally said, so quietly that Dr. Anderson had to lean forward to hear him, "it's pretty pathetic that something intended to be an insult is actually a compliment."

"I'm not sure I follow," Dr. Anderson said, furrowing his brow while leaning back so that he was no longer invading Drew's personal space.

Drew angrily stretched out his shirt so that Dr. Anderson could see the remnants of the so-called hickey.

"Because this is *not* a hickey," Drew spat out. "I'm as likely to get a hickey as you are to, to…" Drew struggled to find an analogy that proved his point. "As you are to put on a tutu and run through downtown Charlotte singing Mary Had a Little Lamb."

"I see," said Dr. Anderson. That was a common refrain of his, whether or not he did see. It was his equivalent of *hmmmm*.

"*This*," Drew said, again stretching out the shirt so that the mark was visible, "is thanks to a pencil --- correction, *pencils* --- being thrown at me in art class."

Dr. Anderson shook his head in disgust. He always seemed shocked to learn that bullying could entail more than words.

"Did you report who threw the pencils?" Dr. Anderson asked.

It was for this reason that Drew had stopped sharing the almost daily incidents of getting shoved or having things thrown at him, not to mention his glasses getting stolen, his backback thrown around like a crueler version of monkey in the middle, with Drew always, always being the monkey, or his books and desk getting vandalized. Because Dr. Anderson didn't get it, even though Drew had explained it to him during their first session, when he'd been referred to him after Mrs. Lewin, the school psychologist, had told his parents she was worried about him and the toll the bullying was taking on him. "It is my professional opinion," she explained, looking at first one, then the other, with her kind, patient eyes, "that Drew needs professional help."

No adults got it. Not his parents, not his teachers, not Mrs. Lewin, nice as she was, and not Dr. Anderson. Definitely not Dr. Anderson. Reporting it didn't do squat. Even if the bullies were punished, it didn't stop. Losing a lab turn or getting a zero for the class activity of the day didn't phase them at all because these were not things they cared about. Even when Josh Manicki got suspended, after he wrote DREW IS GAY in a black sharpie all over Drew's locker, he went after Drew with a vengeance when the suspension was over. Reporting it, Drew had learned the hard way, actually made it worse.

"What's upsetting," Drew said, ignoring Dr. Anderson's question about the pencils, "is that I was actually relieved, *flattered* almost, that Joe thought it was a hickey."

Dr. Anderson nodded.

"You mean, because of the general perception that you are gay."

Yes and no. For sure, part of it was that Drew was sick and tired of the incessant comments about his sexual orientation. All because he had said, back in third grade, when Josh Anderson announced Drew was gay because he had ordered the meatball sub instead of the cheese pizza at lunch that day (who knew that one meal choice over another determined your sexuality?) that he didn't know if he was (he really didn't; he liked both boys and girls, at least when they weren't being mean to him, and he didn't have romantic or sexual feelings for either gender) but that there was nothing wrong with being gay anyway. Not a good move. If you're not slinging around insults of "You're gay," then, well, you *are* gay.

But it was more than that. Drew was about as far from getting a hickey as Dr. Anderson was. It was pathetic that an entire bus singing a chorus of "Drew's got a hickey! Drew's got a hickey!" was actually a move up for him.

And it was that, more than anything else he'd endured, that depressed him. How low was his status, how pathetic was his life, that a welt from a pencil being thrown at him was misconstrued into an insult that actually endowed him with more social clout than he actually had?

Dr. Anderson didn't get it, but then, he rarely did.

CHAPTER TWO

"I can't," Lily said, slamming her locker shut and heading towards the bus lot. "I've got a date."

"With who?" Mike demanded, looking incensed, as if asking Lily out for months -- without success, mind you -- entitled him to be jealous of any other plans she made.

"With whom?" Lily corrected him.

"Hoom? Hoom? Who is he? Is that the new Chinese exchange student dude?" Mike was chasing after Lily as she ran to get on her bus. Bus 362 was always the last one to leave, because Miss Madge liked to finish her cigarette and flirt with the school security officer before pulling out of the Crestdale Middle School parking lot, but Mike didn't need to know that.

Lily saw him standing there, beneath her window, motioning for her to open it, but she acted as stupid as he really was and pretended she didn't understand what he was saying. She waved goodbye and then propped open the biggest textbook she had in her backpack, 8th Grade Geography, shielding herself from her grammar-challenged suitor.

He was such a moron. Lily told her Mom the Mike story to prove her point, that no guy at school could prove as interesting or enjoyable as her Friday night SCRABBLE game with Jeremy, but her Mom wasn't buying it.

"It's just not right, hon," she said, shaking her head and punctuating her point with an exaggerated sigh. "You're a wonderful sister to Jeremy, but you have your own life to live. You are a *teenager* who should be out having fun with other *teenagers*."

"It is so odd," Lily replied, not for the first time, "that you keep pushing me out the door. Samantha and Jessie's moms are doing everything they can to *keep* them from going out. They want them home *more*, not *less.* We have a pretty bizarre role reversal thing going on here."

It was the wrong thing to say.

"That's just it," Sally said, her eyes sad. "You are thirteen years old. You are gorgeous and smart and young. You shouldn't be role reversing with your mother. You should be out there…"

Lily couldn't hear it all over again. "I get it Mom, I get it,' she interrupted. "The first decent offer I get, I'm outa here. Promise."

She quickly took out the SCRABBLE board and racks, realizing with alarm that it was seven forty-two. At seven forty-five it would be time to play SCRABBLE; not a minute before, but not a minute *after* either. Once, and only once, she had failed to have the board ready on time. It wasn't pretty.

"However," she added, plopping down in her chair, "I doubt very much I'm going to get a date as great as Jeremy."

Jeremy shuffled in, his Homer Simpson slippers announcing his arrival with their unmistakable scuffling down the hallway. He had four freshly-sharpened number two pencils held firmly in one hand and the Official SCRABBLE Players Dictionary, Fourth Edition, clasped in the other. He was wearing a pair of gray, elastic-waistband sweatpants and a gray and white striped polo shirt Lily had picked out for him at Old Navy.

"I *am* a great date," he said, having arrived just in time to hear his name being mentioned. "I like being your date, Lily."

Lily got up and gave her brother a kiss on his cheek. "I like being your date too," she said. "And I love our Friday night SCRABBLE games."

"Me too," Jeremy said, eying the clock. Seven forty-four and thirty-two seconds.

Sally began making the hot chocolate. She couldn't serve it until Jeremy had put his first set of tiles on his rack. As with everything else in his life, the timing had to be just right. It was pointless to fight it. She had tried making him see reason, using therapy, bribes, cajoling (*v,* to persuade by flattery) him and even punishment as a means of lessening his obsessive compulsiveness about time and numbers, but to no avail. And she realized, one day when her highly functional autistic son was not very functional at all, was, in fact, banging his head against the window and sobbing because she had tried to make him leave the house before six blue cars had driven by, that her efforts were not only unproductive, they were counterproductive. He was regressing.

If it weren't for her concern about Lily, Sally would have no complaints about the Friday night SCRABBLE games. What parent *wouldn't* love having her two teenaged children choosing to spend time with each other, enjoying each other's company while engaging in a game of intellect and skill? And she loved watching Jeremy play SCRABBLE, because it was a game that was particularly well suited to the way his mind worked. She could almost pretend he was okay; that there was nothing wrong with the way his mind worked in other ways.

"E" Jeremy said, plucking a tile out of the bag at precisely seven forty-five.

"L" Lily said, taking her own tile out. "Looks like you go first. Again."

"I have gone first 22 of the last 34 games we have played," Jeremy concurred. "I went first on October 3rd, October 10th, both times on October 17th, but not on all the games on October 24th, because we played three games that day, it was a Saturday, and...."

"I get it," Lily said, marveling at her brother's phenomenal recall but knowing the litany would go on forever unless she stopped it. She'd lived with Jeremy, who was six years older than she was, her entire life. She'd never known anything but an autistic brother, so you'd think Jeremy's way of thinking and speaking would be old hat, but it wasn't. Lily continued to be in awe of how her brother processed and stored information; how he could multiply nine thousand seventeen and six hundred twelve in his head, in nanoseconds, and could tell you what row they'd sat in during their bus ride to the airport in Cincinnati three years ago, but he couldn't carry on a conversation with the clerk at Harris Teeter or ask Lily how her day was.

Jeremy picked his seven letters and put them on his rack. Then and only then could Sally bring her children their cups of hot cocoa. She saw Jeremy eye the marshmallows and mentally tally them in his head.

"There are seventeen," she reassured him, but she knew he had to count them for himself.

"Seventeen is a prime number," Jeremy announced, after he had ascertained (*v,* to find out something with certainty) that there were, in fact, seventeen marshmallows atop his hot chocolate. "So is fifty-three, four hundred and one and one thousand and thirteen. But seventeen is my favorite."

"Good thing," Lily said, sitting down and blowing on her own cup. "Otherwise we'd have a mighty hard time getting all those marshmallows in there."

"It would have to be a very big cup," Jeremy agreed, not understanding that Lily was joking.

Her mom got it, though, and she winked at Lily.

Jeremy shuffled the seven tiles that were on his rack around, rearranging them rapidly until he was satisfied. He put seven tiles on the board, in quick succession. "R A D I A T E. D is doubled for four, plus six is ten, times two is twenty, plus fifty is seventy," he said.

"You did NOT just start off with a bingo," Lily said, with mock indignation.

"I did," Jeremy said, smiling proudly. "And it's a natural one. A natural bingo. No blanks."

"Allrighty then, rub it in some more," Lily said, marking his score down. There was really no need for her to keep score as well, since Jeremy did it too and she was pretty sure he also kept a mental tally going, but she liked feeling like she was contributing something. She very occasionally won, when all the tiles went her way and she was able to close off the board and block Jeremy's inevitable bingos, but for the most part, she not only lost, but lost handily, and her scorekeeping was sometimes her only source of pride in a game.

Lily was actually a better SCRABBLE player than she realized. Thanks to Jeremy, she knew words she would never have seen or used in everyday 8th grade life, and playing with him couldn't help but convert his opponent into a more strategically savvy (*adj*, shrewd, having keen insight) player. She was also well versed in the rules of the game, because Jeremy had read and memorized the official rule book the North American SCRABBLE Association had sent him, once Sally had plunked down the $25 for an annual membership, and, having done so, playing any other way than with strict adherence to the rules, no matter how obscure and ridiculous, was unfathomable (*adj*, so mysterious or complicated that understanding is impossible). There would be no casual, kitchen-table games in their household. No looking up words in between turns the way Samantha's family did; no taking a word off the board and trying again if it was no good. No, Jeremy and Lily played with an official time clock; challenges came with the risk of losing a turn; and penalties accrued if you went over your allotted twenty-five minutes.

Lily had a U she wanted to dump, since U's were a pain in the butt unless you had a Q on your rack, which she didn't, so she played UPO (*prep,* upon), lining up the U above the T in RADIATE, forming the words UT (*n,* the musical tone C in the French solmization system, now replaced by *do*) and PE (*n,* a Hebrew letter) as well.

When the phone rang a few minutes later, Jeremy was so intent on laying down his third bingo of the night that he didn't bark his usual "NO PHONE!"

There were certain concessions Sally was unwilling to make, and turning off the phone was one of them.

"People have to be able to reach us," she explained. "We can't be cut off from society every time you play SCRABBLE or watch Jeopardy."

Jeopardy was another game at which Jeremy excelled. When she was younger, Lily was obsessed with finding a way to get her big brother on the game show, convinced he'd clean up and set them all up for life with his winnings. She didn't understand that knowing the answers was only part of it. Just the initial chit chat, like Alex Trebec asking each contestant to elaborate on something interesting about themselves ("It says here you once went a whole week eating nothing but chili dogs. Please explain how that came about!") would stop him cold. And the buzzer? Forget about it. Jeremy liked blurting out the answers, and no amount of chastising him for never, ever letting his sister even think about whether she knew the answer (she never even had time to process the question, let alone formulate some kind of answer before he blurted it out) stopped him from yelling it out. Lily knew now that Jeremy couldn't do Jeopardy. He couldn't do a lot of things, even though, in fact, he really *could,* better, in fact, than most people. That's the part that was so gosh darn frustrating, but Lily had come to terms with it because Jeremy had. Jeremy was perfectly content to play Jeopardy in the Mallovari living room and to have no one other than his mother and sister around to be wowed by his SCRABBLE prowess. He seemed oblivious to what he was missing.

"The blank is an S," Jeremy announced, laying down his tiles – all seven of them, for his third bingo of the night – to form the word BARFLIES.

"Hold," Lily said, trying to read his body language. She would never have challenged a word of Jeremy's before, thinking –

erroneously, it turns out -- that playing an intentional phony was beyond him. He played MILITUA so convincingly a few weeks earlier, laying down the tiles with such confidence and with no hint of a smile or his trademark giggle that usually gave him away when he was trying to get away with something, that Lily assumed it was simply one of the millions of words he knew that she didn't. She figured it was some variation of MILITIA and she dutifully wrote down his score.

"That was a phony!" Jeremy announced proudly, clapping his hands in what would surely have seemed like a display of poor sportsmanship in anyone but him. "I played a phony!"

Lily was secretly pleased that duping her was in his repertoire. It showed a certain savvy (*n*, shrewdness and practical knowledge) and degree of social skills she didn't think he possessed.

Jeremy refrained from taking his new tiles, but he looked intently at the clock, knowing that Lily had only one minute to hold him on her time until he could replace the tiles he'd played.

"I challenge," Lily announced, hitting the stop button on the clock.

Jeremy got up with great fanfare.

"Okay Lily, okay, you challenge. Let's go." Jeremy seemed way too happy about the challenge.

They walked to the computer, where Zyzzyva was loaded, and Lily typed in the word.

"Green screen," Jeremy said, again clapping his hands. "I win. The play is good."

"I thought you were trying to trick me again," Lily said, laughing. "Barflies, huh? That just sounds like a made-up word."

"BARFLIES, noun, plural, a drinker who frequents bars," Jeremy said, taking on the tone of a robotic computer. "I could also have made the blank a B and played FLABBIER, adjective, flabby, flaccid, lacking firmness; or an E for AFERBILE, adjective, having no fever; or BALEFIRE, noun, a bonfire; or FIREABLE, also with the E, adjective, to project by discharging from a gun; or an L for FIREBALL, noun, a luminous meteor."

He paused to take a breath, during which time Lily and Sally exchanged looks of incredulity (*n*, a state or feeling of disbelief). They knew Jeremy; they lived with Jeremy; but they still found themselves, at moments like this, feeling like observers of an exotic creature at the zoo.

"But BARFLIES was the best," Jeremy said. "95 points because of the triple word score. FLABBIER was 83 points. AFERBILE was 97 points but it set up the double double. BALEFIRE was…"

Lily put her hand on his. "I have no doubt it was the best play, Jer," she said.

"Now I'm starting your clock again because it's your turn."

Lily had a few good turns too, playing the X in the triple letter score with an I next to it and an A above it, to form the words AX and XI (*n,* a Greek letter) for 50 points and she even bingoed once herself with EQUATED (*v, past tense,* to make equal) for 86 points, but Jeremy still won by over 200 points.

"Congrats," Lily said, sticking out her hand. "I'm shocked you were able to pull out a victory tonight."

The comment was for her mom's enjoyment; sarcasm was lost on Jeremy.

"I was ahead the entire game," Jeremy said. "And here," he pointed to the spot on the scoresheet when there were fewer than three turns left before the end of the game, "it was mathematically impossible for you to win. It is not shocking that I won. Not at all."

"No, it's not, " Lily agreed, getting up and giving him a big hug.

"I'm going to go analyze our game," Jeremy said, taking the score sheet with him and heading over to the computer, where Zyzzyva and hours of anagramming awaited him.

"You do that," Lily said, helping him push back his chair. "And I'm going to…"

"Clean up!" Jeremy announced with glee. "Loser cleans up."

CHAPTER THREE

"Oh, I wondered what those said." Drew smoothed out the crumpled flyer Aidan pulled out of his back pocket. "You must have found the only one that wasn't vandalized."

"Yeah, Mr. Springer should know better than to post 'DO YOU LIKE TO SPELL?' all over the school. I mean, that's like *begging* kids to abuse you."

"Besides," Drew added, seeing that the flyer was, in fact, an invitation to join Randolph Middle School's first-ever SCRABBLE Club, "being a good speller does not necessarily translate into being a good SCRABBLE player."

"Yeah, but it's a pretty good way of weeding out, oh, about 99.9 percent of the Randolph student body."

"Point," Drew agreed.

"I'll go if you go," Aidan offered, slurping down the last of his chocolate milk.

"It depends when it is," Drew replied. "I've got National Academic League on Mondays, Chess Club on Tuesday mornings, Hebrew School on Wednesdays, Math Counts on Fridays and…"

"So drop one of your geeky clubs for…."

"For an even geekier club?" Drew chimed in, laughing. They both knew SCRABBLE Club, while a sure-fire way to be branded a king nerd, was no lower than any of their other activities, and would probably attract the same flock of RMS nerds that the other "There-Is-No-Sports-Scholarship-In-My-Future" clubs did. Aidan shared Drew's pond-scum social status; he knew that poking fun at Drew was poking fun at himself.

Drew weighed down the corner of the flyer with his half-eaten jello bowl (he'd stopped eating it once he no longer felt sure that the unidentified green blobs in it were, in fact, grapes) and read it more carefully.

DO YOU LIKE TO SPELL?
DO YOU LOVE WORD GAMES?

Did you know that "oe" means "a whirlwind off the Faeroe
Islands?"
Or that "ka" means "an Egyptian spirit?"
Do you know that "z" and "q" are worth 10 points?

If you answered yes to any of these questions,
then you need to join
Randolph Middle School's

SCRABBLE CLUB!

We will meet on Thursday mornings at 7:30 am.
We will learn the official rules of the National SCRABBLE
Association,
play fun and challenging word games to increase our
vocabularies and our SCRABBLE-playing skills, and, best of
all, we will

PLAY SCRABBLE GAMES & COMPETITIONS!

All students are welcome, including those who have never
played before.
If you are interested in joining the SCRABBLE Club,
See Mr. Springer in Room 213.

"Mr. Springer said he's counting on us to come," Aidan added.

Both boys had forged a close bond with their teacher, who had created a special, accelerated Latin class just for them because they had moved at such a fast clip when he first taught them Latin in sixth grade.

"Sure he is," Drew agreed. "Because you need two players to make it official and he knows no one else will show."

But Drew was wrong. That first morning, eleven kids showed up. Seven sixth graders, two seventh graders, and Drew and Aidan.

"Why can't we meet *after* school?" Irwin Mu asked, yawning, as he plopped down at one of the tables Mr. Springer had set up with a SCRABBLE board.

"Because we'd all get beat up," Drew muttered.

Rather than chastising him for his negativity, Mr. Springer chuckled in agreement.

"Yeah, the bullies will leave you alone at this hour," he said, winking at Drew, "because they're too lazy to drag their butts into school this early."

"So who's ready to take me on?" Jennifer Espionza asked, dumping her tile bag on the board. All of the plastic tile squares cascaded out in a noisy clatter.

"I'll bet you a week's worth of desserts at lunch that I can beat you by over 100 points," Mark Mallard said, plopping down across from her. "Bring it."

"Whoa, hold on there, you SCRABBLE maniacs," Mr. Springer said, holding up his hand.

He took out a huge, oversized SCRABBLE board mounted on foam board and propped it on an easel.

"First we're going to go over some of the basics, to make sure we're all on the same page."

"Or on the same SCRABBLE board," Drew muttered.

"Ooh, SCRABBLE Club humor," Aidan said. "Gotta love it."

Mr. Springer shot them a look.

"First off, let me see a show of hands for everyone who has played SCRABBLE before," Mr. Springer raised his own hand to lead the way, as if it was a difficult concept to grasp unless he modeled what to do.

Aidan and Drew raised their hands, as did Jennifer and Irwin and two of the sixth graders. Surprisingly, no one else did, including Mark Mallard, who had just bet Jennifer that he would beat her by 100 points.

Drew marveled at that kind of bravado. He sure didn't have it. He never thought he had aced a test, even though he often did, and he never thought he'd win a chess game or get the NAL question right or score well on the Math Counts problem, even though he almost always did.

Dr. Anderson asked him, at his first or second session, why that was.

"The empirical evidence is that you're a remarkable young man," Dr. Anderson commented, shuffling through the papers that Mrs. Lewin had sent over from school. "So why do you think it is that *you* don't seem to think so?"

Drew stared at his shoes, as if his untied laces were suddenly worthy of intense scrutiny. "You try getting picked last at every gym class scrimmage," he felt like saying, "or have no one ever ask you to be on their team at recess or call you to go to the movies or to a birthday party, except for the few geeks who are even bigger losers than you are. It doesn't exactly boost your self-esteem." But instead he just grunted and said, "I dunno." He decided that he had the right to just as many *I dunnos* as Dr. Anderson had to his *Hmmms* and *I sees.*

"I wonder if this low opinion of yourself isn't somehow linked to how others perceive you," Dr. Anderson continued.

"So if I just walk into school tomorrow thinking I'm cool and popular, that's how I'll be treated?" Drew asked, his voice dripping with sarcasm. Dr. Anderson's simplistic solution infuriated him.

But Drew grudgingly admired Mark's bravado – bragging that you could beat someone at a game you've never played before, that took something Drew didn't have.

"Okay, at the risk of boring you seasoned SCRABBLE players," Mr. Springer continued, "we're going to spend today going over the basics."

"Oh joy," Drew thought to himself. "And for this I got up early?"

"What's the object of the game of SCRABBLE?" Mr. Springer asked the group.

"To win," Mark yelled out. "Duh."

Cecelia Weng raised her hand.

"To form words," she said, when Mr. Springer nodded at her. "And to build on the words that are already on the board."

"Great," Mr. Springer smiled at her. "You got it." Turning to Mark, he added, "And how is it that you win at this word-building game?"

"By scoring the most points," Mark replied, not uttering the word "Duh" this time but implying it with the way he answered the question. "The longer the word, the more points you get."

"Not necessarily," Mr. Springer corrected him. "That would be true if all the letters were worth the same amount of points, but they're not."

"So you make words and whoever makes the ones with the most points wins?" Mark asked, trying to move the chitchat portion of SCRABBLE Club along so they could get to actually playing a game.

"Yes, that's pretty much it in a nutshell," Mr. Springer agreed. "But look down at your boards and tell me how else you can get points in this game."

Drew knew, but he wasn't about to volunteer the answer. Even among nerds, Drew was usually branded the King Nerd, a loser among losers, and he was determined to give them as little fodder as possible to anoint (*v*, to install somebody officially or ceremonially in a position or office) him the low man on the totem poll at SCRABBLE Club.

"Cecelia, illuminate us," Mr. Springer nodded in her direction, adding a smile of encouragement since speaking in front of anyone – even her own parents – was a struggle for her. Shy didn't even begin to cover it.

"There are different colored squares that increase the value of your letter or word," she said, so softly that Mr. Springer repeated it for everyone to hear.

"So think of the SCRABBLE board like a big puzzle," Mr. Springer advised everyone. "*Where* you place a word is *as* important – if not *more* important – than *what* the word is." He paused and surveyed the group. "Does everyone get that?"

Nods all around, mainly because everyone was itchy to play.

"Okay, now let's talk about some of the rules," Mr. Springer said, passing out a sheet labeled SCRABBLE RULES while everyone groaned.

"Hey, if you went out for the soccer team, you wouldn't just go out and play against South Charlotte Middle on your first day of practice," Mr. Springer admonished them. "I assure you we'll be playing lots of SCRABBLE, but…"

Mark interrupted him. "But Mr. S, at least you get to kick the soccer ball around on the first day of practice. You may not be ready for a match against another school, but you do get to *play*. Can we please just *play*?"

"I tell you what," Mr. Springer compromised, although it was actually what he'd planned all along, "we will all play a game together so that we can learn as we go."

Groans from most of the group. Never inject the word "learn" into a middle school activity if you want an enthusiastic response.

"It'll be all of you against me on this board," Mr. Springer said, pointing to the big board on the easel.

Cheers and hollering. "You're going *down*, Mister S!" Mark yelled out.

All of the members of the RMS SCRABBLE Club pulled their chairs close as Lucy, a nervous sixth grader, pulled out their first set of letters and placed them on their rack.

"Hey, it's not *her* fault," Drew muttered, noticing Lucy was fighting back tears when her draw was met by boos and groans.

He surveyed the seemingly impossible collection of letters on their rack:

V Q R X L O N

"What happens when you can't make a move at all?" Mohammed asked.

"Yeah, can we trade in the ones we don't like?" Brandon inquired.

"Like all of them?" Jennifer chimed in.

"You can trade in any or all of your letters," Mr. Springer replied. "But that counts as your turn."

Mark began gathering up the tiles.

"Just a minute," Drew yelled out, with a forcefulness that surprised everyone, including himself. "We didn't agree to trade in," he added, deliberately softening his tone. "It's not like we don't have a play."

"Okay, Genius Boy," Mark replied, throwing the letters back down on the table. "Let me see you make a word with *these*."

"I actually see two words," Drew said quietly. He motioned for everyone to come in close, then whispered, "L-O-X and V-O-X."

"I've had lox on my bagel at Phil's Deli" Lucy piped up, then looked crestfallen and back to being on the verge of tears when everyone shushed her because she spoke loudly enough for Mr. Springer to hear.

"Nah, that's a proper noun," Mark said, unwilling to concede that there was a word he'd missed in the pile he was ready to throw back in the bag.

"Nope, it's good," Aidan said, patting Drew on the back. "Good find, Drew."

"But vox is even better," Drew whispered. "It's more points, since the V is worth 4 points, plus the V is harder to use so it's better for us if we get rid of it while we can."

Everyone but Mark nodded in agreement.

"Lucy, if you guys have agreed," Mr. Springer instructed, using his Camp Counselor voice, "then bring your word up here to put it on the board. The first play of the game has to cover up this pink square with a star in it in the middle, which serves as a double word score square."

Biting her lower lip and acting as if she were carrying a toxic substance, Lucy carried the letters over to the board and affixed (*v,* to attach; to connect as an associated part) them on the three middle squares.

"Vox," Mr. Springer said, acting surprised, as if he hadn't heard their heated discussion. "Great start. How many points is that?"

"Twenty-six" several voices cried out.

"Okey-dokey," Mr. Springer put their score up on the flip chard next to the SCRABBLE Board.

He also put his tiles up on the flip chart so that everyone could see them. "This is supposed to be a *learning* exercise," he said in response to the quizzical looks sent his way. "I wouldn't share my letters with my opponent – or *opponents,* as the case may be – in a real game, but for the purposes of this exercise I'd rather have you all see them so that you can be part of my thought process."

"Man, you've got good letters," Brandon exclaimed. "I see a whole bunch of words."

"Me too," David, a 7th grader in baggy shorts and a Charlotte Knights shirt, said excitedly. David's mom had signed him up for the club because it allowed her to drop him off at school an hour and a half early, which meant she could skip the traffic on Providence Road on her way in to work. David had never even heard of SCRABBLE before and was none too enthused, but his mom let him know this was not one of those decisions he got to weigh in on.

Mr. Springers letters were A   E   B   T   I   R   L.

"Now remember," Mr. Springer cautioned the group, "it's important to consider the tiles on your rack in conjunction with the board. You can't think of them in a vacuum."

David looked downright confused, as if the words he had found no longer made sense.

"I'm just saying that you need to not only think of words, but figure out where to put them on the board. Or use your tiles to form words incorporating the tiles that are already on the board."

"Like putting E and T after the V for *vet*?" Irwin asked.

"Ooh, I've got one that's even better," Mohammed yelled out. "Boiler, putting the B above the O in VOX."

"What does VOX mean, anyway?" Jennifer asked.

"It's another word for voice," Aidan and Drew said together. Smiling sheepishly at Mr. Springer, they added, "It's Latin."

"So foreign words are good?" Mohammed said. "Then I can play things in Arabic? Sweet."

"Only certain foreign words are good," Mr. Springer explained.

He held up a small red book. "This," he said, handing it to Cecelia and motioning her to pass it around, "is the SCRABBLE Players Official Dictionary, Volume IV. If the word is in there, it's acceptable. If not, then you can't use it. I can't say it always makes sense what's acceptable and what's not, but that's what we've got to go with."

"We've got to learn all those words?" David asked, looking dumbfounded.

"No, no, I don't even know half of them," Mr. Springer reassured him. "Only the top players in the country have the whole dictionary memorized. But there are certain words I do expect you to memorize."

Another round of groans.

Ignoring the comments about how clubs were supposed to be about having fun and were *not* supposed to involve homework, Mr. Springer took out a large manila envelope and pulled out a stack of laminated sheets.

"This," he said, handing the pile to David, and motioning to him to take one and pass them on, "is your very own cheat sheet. I've even punched holes in it so that you can keep it in your binder."

"Beast," Aidan said, trying to sound hip, as he surveyed the list of two- and three- letter words, short words using X and J, and good vowel dumps. "This will come in very handy."

"So who sees what letters we can put on either side of the X that's on the board?" Mr. Springer asked, once everyone had had a few moments to survey their cheat sheets.

"You can put the O on top of the X for OX," Jennifer volunteered.

"Or you can put an I after the X for xi," Mark yelled out. "What the heck is exi?"

"It's pronounced zee," Mr. Springer replied.

"That's really a word?" Lucy said, no longer pouty. "Seriously?"

"Yup, there are all sorts of funky words on here. Words even those of us who love words have never heard of, let alone used. But if they're on here, they're good."

"So what's exi, I mean, zee *mean?"* Mark asked again.

"Well, I happen to know what it means," Mr. Springer replied, "as does Drew, I'm willing to bet." He nodded at Drew, who looked both pleased and embarrassed at the same time. "But if I didn't, and if you don't know if something's a word in the future, you're going to head over to any of the computers here in the Media Center." Mr. Springer motioned for everyone to head to one of the many computers stationed around the room. "You see that little blue Z icon at the bottom? That's called Zyzzyva, and it's a word program I have installed on every computer in here."

After everyone clicked on it, as instructed, Mr. Springer told them to click on the dictionary icon in the upper left-hand corner.

"Now type in xi," he commanded. "And what do you see?"

"It's a Greek letter," Brandon yelled out.

"What's the *n* mean?" David asked.

"That it's a noun," Jennifer shot back, muttering "Duh!" under her breath.

"This is a great way to learn the definitions of words, but you can't use it during a game unless you are challenging a word." Mr. Springer explained how challenges work, and the glazed look he saw staring back at him on several kids' faces let him know he was quickly approaching information overload.

"So let's get back to my turn," he said. "Using the cheat sheets, especially the two-letter word list, who can think of my best play?"

"You already said it," Mark said, "Xi or OX, take your pick."

"That's good, but it's not the best. Always try to form as many words as possible."

"I thought you could only make one word per turn?" Mark shot back, frustrated with the rules that seemed to keep changing and getting more complex with each turn.

"Drew, come up here and show everyone what I mean," Mr. Springer instructed.

Drew reluctantly got up and walked to the flip board. He picked up the B, A, I and L to form the word bail (*v,* to transfer property temporarily) and put the B above the O in VOX and the A above the X.

"Oh, I forgot about ax," Mark acknowledged.

"Not just that," Mr. Springer said, patting Drew on the back as he returned to his seat, "but Drew formed three separate words with this play. What are they?"

"Bo," Aidan said having already run back to the Zyzzyva on his computer, "which means a pal." He turned away from the computer and looked back up at the board. "*And* AX and BAIL for a total of twenty-one points because the A is on the double letter square."

"Exactamundo," Mr. Springer said, "which I think you'll all agree is the best play."

Even Mark grudgingly nodded.

Drew wondered if *exactamundo* was an acceptable SCRABBLE word. He doubted it.

"Now could we have started our word above or below the V?" Mr. Springer asked.

"No, because there's no two-letter V word," David replied, after scouring the 2-letter word list several times.

"Right you are," Mr. Springer said, and David beamed. Drew suspected David wasn't accustomed to being told he was right very often, at least not within the confines of Randolph Middle School.

"And that," Mr. Springer said, "is all we have time for today."

More groans.

"Man, two turns and that's it? We barely started, Mr. S!" Mark complained.

"Pack everything up before you go," Mr. Springer said. "And I promise next week we'll get straight to the games. Get here on time, find your assigned opponent – I'll have a list at the start of club each week up here on the flip board – and you should be able to get an entire game in. Promise."

Drew wondered if anyone else was mentally exhausted. It was a lot to take in, and he couldn't imagine how much it was to process for the kids who had never even played before. Maybe it was just that his brain wasn't used to being in demand this early in the morning. Then again, he knew plenty of kids at Randolph whose brains would probably short-circuit from being used at all, no matter what time of day.

CHAPTER FOUR

Four more laps to go. Lily hoped Jeremy could make it that long because she really wanted to run three miles today.

She waved as she passed him but he didn't see her. He was staring straight ahead, with a vacant stare that Lily knew was anything *but* vacant. What went on in her brother's head was almost always at a level far more advanced than what her brain was capable of processing; Lily knew that with the same certainty that she knew he would also be absolutely lost without her. People were always surprised and flummoxed (*v*, to confuse, to mix up mentally) by the contrast between Jeremy's intellectual capacity and his social skills, but to Lily it made perfect sense.

She had read all the books on autism her mom had checked out of the South Charlotte Library for her, when Lily's questions and insistence that Jeremy could and would get better had made her mother feel that she needed the clinical experts to intercede on her behalf, but none of them really got it. Not in a way that really described Jeremy. What Lily concluded, and it was so simple, really, was that it came down to an inability to multi-task. Every one of Jeremy's brain cells, of which there were a multitude (*n*, a very large number of things or people), was devoted to the task at hand, whether it was memorizing word lists or train schedules or the names of Ancient Greek Gods, leaving not a single brain cell behind to devote to social interaction or processing anything else that was going on around him. That's what made him so amazingly good at the things he was good at; he could devote himself to them one hundred percent. But that meant that nothing, and in Jeremy's case, it really was *nothing,* was left to handle seemingly simple tasks like accepting that the Matthews Harris Teeter was all out of Cinnamon Life and that no amount of carrying on in the deficient cereal aisle was going to change that.

This cluelessness did have its advantages, though, because it also meant Jeremy was oblivious (*adj,* unaware of or paying no attention to somebody or something) to the reactions people had to him. Lily was hurt or miffed (*adj,* annoyed, troubled) almost every day by the way someone looked at him or snickered, but not Jeremy. His feelings never got hurt because those expressions of disdain (*n,* scorn or contempt) or pity never registered with him. Even well-meaning folks, those who understood that he couldn't help himself when he talked too loudly in a restaurant or stared straight ahead instead of looking at them when they greeted him, infuriated Lily with their pity. She wanted to shake them sometimes, the nice folks, the ones who seemed to be saying, "Oh, poor you. Oh, poor him. What a sad state of affairs," and yell, "He has talents you couldn't dream of possessing! He's amazingly kind and funny and he doesn't need or deserve your pity!" But Jeremy never knew that he needed defending. He was unaware that he was being judged.

Jeremy gave her a big thumbs up when she lapped him again. He was mesmerized (*adj,* enthralled, fascinated) with the iPod Aunt Nicole gave him for his birthday, which Lily figured was as much a gift for *her* and her mom as it was for *him* because it kept him so entertained and happy. Jeremy, like most autistics, loved repetition; if he liked something; he wanted it times 100, no variations. So being able to program his iPod so that his favorite Beatles song, *Hey Jude,* could repeat itself 17 times in a row, well, that was nirvana (*n,* a blessed state in Buddhism) for her brother. Lily had tried showing him the joys of the shuffle feature, where he could enjoy a random selection of songs from the Beatles albums he had programmed on his iPod, but that was a disaster. Jeremy hated the uncertainty and surprise: he liked being in control of what was coming next. If the order was different than the last time he'd heard the album (and of course he had them all memorized categorically) then he was thrown. Listening to the same song over and over would drive Lily batty, but she had long since learned that imposing what made *her* happy on her big brother was foolish and counterproductive.

Sally Mallovari needed to learn that lesson as far as Lily was concerned.

She had grudgingly dropped her children off at the Y, but she wasn't happy about it.

"You should go out for track and run with a coach and kids your age instead of constantly looking over your shoulder to check on your brother," Sally admonished her daughter. She knew it was a losing battle, but she couldn't resist saying something practically every time she drove Lily and Jeremy to the Y. "Jeremy and I can get our exercise walking around the neighborhood while you're at track practice."

"No, I walk the track with Lily," Jeremy corrected her. "Mondays, Wednesdays and Fridays. That's what we do before dinner. I walk the track with Lily."

"Yeah, Mom, it's a win win," Lily agreed, bending down to tie Jeremy's shoes. "Just enjoy your alone time and come back for us at the usual time. We're good."

She shot her mom a big grin and headed down the grassy slope towards the track, holding Jeremy's elbow to steady him.

It had taken Lily months to get Jeremy to be able to walk by himself while she ran. At first, he'd panic when she took off, failing to appreciate that she was circling the track and would be back with him in about three minutes. He'd also tried to run alongside her, but coordination was not one of his strong suits and he slowed her down so much that it defeated the purpose. The iPod helped immensely, keeping him distracted as he plodded along, while she ran and kept a close eye on him as she circled the track, looking for any signs of distress or indications that she needed to intervene on his behalf.

Lily was always ready to defend her big brother; to protect him from what she often perceived as a cruel, uncompromising world. People her age were so quick to judge; and prone to whisper or outright laugh at him simply because he didn't follow the same social rules that they did. Just last week, when Jeremy had loudly announced, "Look Lily, the Beatles!" after spotting a shirt with Abbey Road on it at Target, several shoppers looked up and stared, and Lily heard a teenaged girl tell her boyfriend (the two had been smooching among the leisure wear just minutes earlier, making much more of a spectacle of themselves than Jeremy did), "Keep it down, retard. It's just a shirt."

What Sally failed to understand was that Lily couldn't simply turn off the protector switch. And it wasn't just Jeremy whom Lily was protecting. When her dad left, Lily worried that at any moment her mom would leave too. She'd heard all the fights about Jeremy, and even though *he* seemed oblivious to the stress he was placing on his parents' marriage, Lily, only six, got it loud and clear. She knew it was Jeremy, sweet, lovable and clueless Jeremy, who had driven her dad away. He was a lot of work, this brother of hers, and even though she now knew that her mom was nothing like her dad, that she would never desert them or give up simply because it was hard, or something she hadn't bargained for, Lily knew her mom had it tough. She never complained, she went out of her way, in fact, to make things cheery and nice and as normal as possible, but she was always so tired, and watching Jeremy, working with Jeremy, placating (*v,* to soothe or mollify) Jeremy, it took a lot out of her. Sally had gone on exactly two dates in the years since Lily's dad had taken off, and Lily suspected her mom had pretty much resigned herself to being a single mom --- and a single *person*-- the rest of her life. Jeremy was a lot to take on, and Sally had tired of even trying to bring someone new into the picture. If Jeremy's own biological father couldn't hack it, couldn't deal with the burden and time commitment a child with autism put on the family, then how could she expect someone new to deal with it?

So serving as her brother's buffer to the outside world was as much about her mom as it was about Jeremy. Lily knew she was pretty much the only person who could lighten her mom's load, and she was determined to do that as much as possible.

A group of about seven runners were stretching, ready to head out on a group run, and they momentarily blocked Lily's view of her brother. She ran a few more strides and when she was finally able to spot him she saw that he was not alone.

Lily couldn't hear the conversation, but a group of boys had surrounded him and Jeremy appeared to be holding their soccer ball. Their body language was not friendly.

"Jeremy, I'm coming!" Lily yelled, dodging the three women who were walking side by side, blocking every lane, and then finding herself momentarily stuck behind a woman pushing her twins in a stroller.

Jeremy didn't look up. *Dang it, he must still have his iPod on,* Lily thought.

Before she could reach him, the nice man with the Red Sox baseball cap she'd seen running several times before – she'd noticed him because he was one of the few people who neither stared at Jeremy nor looked away – said something to the soccer boys. They hesitated, he said something else, and they then backed away.

By the time Lily got there, panting from her sprint, the Red Sox man had positioned himself between the soccer boys and Jeremy and was simply walking alongside him.

"Hey there," he said to Lily, while she crossed her arms above her head and tried to get her breath back. "Everything's cool. No worries. We just need to get these boys back their soccer ball."

Lily almost laughed at the absurdity of it all. Jeremy was in the zone, as she and her mom liked to say. He was happily listening to *Hey Jude*, probably the fifteenth rendition of it, and was oblivious to the commotion around him. He did not even seem to be aware that he was holding a soccer ball, or that the owners of the ball were glaring at him with their hands on their hips.

"How did he end up with the ball?" Lily finally managed to ask, once she was able to breathe again.

"They kicked it over here." Turning to the boys, whom the Red Sox man appeared to know, he added, "On purpose."

The boys started to protest but the Red Sox man held up his hand. "Save it." Turning back to Lily, he added, "And he just picked it up and kept walking. It was the darndest thing."

"He probably just saw it as something in his way," Lily said. "He can be very single-minded."

Somehow, the Red Sox man did not need to be told that Jeremy was autistic or that it had to be Lily to get the ball back. He seemed to intuitively (*adv,* instinctively) know that Jeremy was capable of creating a scene.

"Jer," Lily said, stepping in front of him so that he could see her, "take off your iPod." She also motioned for him to remove his headphones in case he couldn't hear her.

Jeremy smiled broadly at the sight of his sister. He put the soccer ball under one arm and took his headphones off with his free hand.

"Look Lily," Jeremy exclaimed. "I found a ball."

"Yes, you did," Lily said. "But it doesn't belong to us so we have to give it back."

"Is it yours?" Jeremy asked the Red Sox man. "I like your Red Sox hat. I'm a Red Sox fan. They won the World Series in 2007 and 2004. Before that they hadn't won it in 86 years. Not since 1918. The Yankess have won it 27 times. They won it in 1923, 1927, 1928, 1936, 1937..."

"Jeremy," Lily interrupted him, oblivious to the looks of awe and consternation (*n,* a feeling of bewilderment and dismay, often caused by something unexpected) Jeremy's litany (*n,* a long and repetitive list of things) of World Series dates had elicited. "That's baseball, but this is a *soccer* ball and we need to give it back to those boys over there so that they can keep playing soccer with it. It belongs to them."

"I don't play soccer," Jeremy said, shaking his head.

"No, you don't," Lily agreed, gently removing the ball from him.

Handing it to the Red Sox man, she asked, "Would you mind returning it to those jerks for me? I'm afraid of what I'll say if I do it myself."

"No problem," he said, winking at her. "But I actually know them so if you don't mind I'll have them come here to retrieve the ball themselves. They have something *they'd* like to say to you both."

"I'm Elliot, by the way," he said, extending his hand beyond the soccer ball.

"Well, thanks for your help, Elliot," Lily said, shaking his hand.

"And this is?" Elliott asked, turning to Jeremy.

"I'm Jeremy," Jeremy said. "Lily is my sister. I'm Lily's brother. I'm Jeremy. And I don't play soccer."

"Neither do I," Elliott said, stepping off the track onto the grass. Lily and Jeremy, who was holding Lily's hand, did the same.

When the boys approached, having seen Elliott wave them over, they looked like dogs who have been caught eating off the table.

"Hey, Mister Springer, can we have our ball now?" the tall one with hair that practically covered his eyes asked.

"Not until you apologize," Elliot Springer said.

Another boy, who looked like he was the tall boy's brother, stepped forward.

Looking at the ground, he mumbled, "I'm sorry we kicked the ball at you. It was mean."

Jeremy was looking down the track and mumbling Red Sox and Yankees statistics.

"What's *wrong* with him," another boy, sporting a Randolph Middle School soccer shirt, asked.

Lily felt like belting him. She hated when people asked that. And it wasn't just kids. The Harris Teeter cashier, the waitress at Phil and Tony's, even one of her teachers had asked variations of what was wrong with her brother. It made Lily feel like he was some sort of defective merchandise, like she was supposed to answer, "Oh, his thingamabob doesn't fit right so we're going to return him for a better model."

"Nothing's *wrong* with him," Lily replied, seething. "He is autistic."

"Autis *what?*" a third boy asked with a decidedly Hispanic accent.

"Autistic," Elliot Springer interjected. "And don't worry about not knowing what it means because all four of you will be researching it and writing me a one-page essay about autism tonight. I expect it on my desk first thing tomorrow morning or we'll all be having a little chat with Mrs. Villroy."

"Oh man," the tall kid groaned. "I have a ton of homework already tonight."

"Well then, you might want to curtail your soccer game and go get started on it," Elliot said, handing back the soccer ball.

"And you, Miguel," Elliot said, leaning down to address the youngest member of the group. "I have a special essay assignment for you."

Miguel looked anything but pleased.

"What does it say above my blackboard?"

"Be kind to one another," Miguel mumbled, looking down at the grass.

"This is my sister. Lily. And I am her brother," Jeremy repeated, loudly. "This is my sister, Lily. And I am her brother."

Miguel looked up, alarmed. It was clear to everyone that Jeremy was getting agitated.

As Lily calmed him down, talking to him in a soothing tone about what they'd be having for dinner that night, Miguel quickly agreed to write his essay about the sign in his teacher's classroom.

"I'm a teacher at Randolph Middle School," Elliot explained to Lily, once the boys had run off, soccer ball in hand. "And those are some of my students. I apologize sincerely for their behavior. Rest assured they will think long and hard about how they acted."

"No biggie," Lily said, even though it was. For some inexplicable reason, she felt on the verge of tears. "We're used to it."

"It's almost time for Jeopardy," Jeremy said, sounding frantic. "We can't be late for Jeopardy. I always watch Jeopardy while Mom makes dinner. Mom picks us up and we get home in time for Jeopardy." He was looking at his watch in a panic, realizing that the schedule was off.

Lily hadn't realized how the soccer ball incident had delayed them. Where was her mom? She scoured the track and the spot where she usually met them by the water fountain, but no mom.

"Oh geez, my mom is late," Lily whispered to Elliott. "And late is not something Jeremy deals with well."

"Do you want to borrow my cell phone to see where she is?" Elliott asked.

"Yes, thank you," Lily said gratefully. "It's okay, Jer, we'll get home in time for Jeopardy, I promise," she told her brother, with far more confidence than she felt, while Elliott handed her his phone.

At first Lily thought she'd misdialed.

"Hello?" a man's voice said.

"Um, I must have the wrong number," Lily said. "Sorry."

"Are you trying to reach Sally, um,," the man sounded like he was reading something. "Sally Mallovari?".

What the?

"Yes, I am," Lily said, stroking Jeremy's hand to keep him calm. "Who are you?"

"I'm a paramedic with Charlotte Mecklenburg County, Ma'am. I'm afraid Ms. Mallovari's been in an accident. We're transferring her to Presbyterian Hospital right now."

Lily looked at Jeremy, who was humming the Jeopardy theme song while rocking back and forth, and tried to absorb what she'd just been told without letting it show on her face.

" And you are?" the paramedic asked.

"I'm her daughter," Lily said, feeling nauseous. "Is she... um, how bad is it?"

"The injuries are not life-threatening," the paramedic assured her, his tone softening once he realized he was speaking with a child. "Is there someone else we can call? Like your father?"

"No," Lily said. "There's no one else."

CHAPTER FIVE

"You'll see," Mara said, ruffling her son's red curls. "You'll have a growth spurt and you'll sprout up overnight." She put a straw in the pineapple and kiwi smoothie she'd made Drew and placed it before him, then sat down and joined him at the kitchen table. "You'll come down to breakfast in the morning and I'll have to look *up* at you and go out and buy you all new clothes."

Drew slurped down the smoothie, both because it was tasty and because doing so precluded (*v,* to make impossible by previous action) him from having to respond. He didn't feel any need to tower over his mom -- Big whoop. She was all of 5'2" – but he fantasized daily about being able to look down on Matt Santoni. How friggin' awesome would it be to show up at school one day and tap him on his huge, oversized shoulder and watch the fear and disbelief cross his face as the realization that Drew Founts-Hiltone – the little nerdy twerp who was so easy to bully and terrorize – was no longer quite so little?

But Drew knew it was more than just his size at play. There were other small kids at school – kids like the Tomlinson twins, who looked like they still belonged in elementary school, and Ben Fulsom, who was even smaller than Drew despite the fact that he was repeating the 8th grade – but they didn't get picked on. At least not the way Drew did, so much so that it was an unrelenting (*adj,* unyielding or unswerving in determination or resolve) part of his day. There was something about him, Drew knew, that cried out, "Pick on me!" Something within him that served as an invitation to anyone who needed to use him as fodder (*n,* people or things regarded as the necessary but expendable ingredient that makes a system or scheme work) for their own social status. But Matt Santoni was the worst. There were a few times when he'd smacked Drew with a towel in the locker room or licked his lips while suggestively whispering, "Hey, gay boy" when passing him and there'd been no one around to see it. It was as if tormenting Drew was so much a part of his DNA, so ingrained into his natural response to Drew, that bullying him was instinctive. He didn't need an audience to admire him in the act.

It was this aspect of Matt's bullying that Drew found the most disturbing and bewildering. In addition to the "Why me?' lament that was shared by all victims, Drew also found himself wondering, in an almost clinical and detached way, "Why *here*?" Why *now*?" He had tried describing it to Dr. Anderson, back when he thought that doing everything that was asked of him in his sessions with the shrink would put a speedier end to the humiliation of having to go see a shrink in the first place. *Tried* being the operative term since Dr. Anderson entirely missed the point of Drew's analogy (*n,* a comparison between two things that are similar in some respects, often used to help explain something or make it easier to understand) of a tree falling in a forest with no one around to see it fall. Or hear it fall. Drew couldn't remember which it was, but it didn't matter, the point was that the tree still fell, even if no one saw it *or* heard it. "Matt is intent on making life hell for me," Drew marveled, "even if none of his football buddies are there to egg him on." He sighed, looking up at Dr. Anderson for sympathy, but Dr. Anderson was bent over his notebook, scribbling away. "I am his proverbial punching bag, and he needs to punch the bag every chance he gets, even if no one is around to admire him punching the bag." Even now, removed from it, Drew found himself shaking with frustration at the futility of it all; the utter injustice of being teased and tormented with absolutely no social capital at stake.

Dr. Anderson finally looked up.

"And how does that make you feel?" Dr. Anderson asked.

"*Really?*" Drew wanted to shoot back at him. "That's the best you've got? College and medical school and whatever else they make you do to earn all those fancy degrees that are framed and displayed all over your office, and the best you've got for me is '*And how does that make you feel?*'"

"How do you *think* it makes me feel?" he wanted to shoot back.

"It sucks," Drew said.

"You have a lot of anger built up," Dr. Anderson commented, while Drew seethed (*v,* to be in a state of extreme emotion, especially unexpressed anger) in the plush leather chair across from him.

Was this guy for real? Was this really what he was paid to do? Ask inane (*adj,* empty, insubstantial, or void) questions and state the obvious?

"Have you ever tried expressing how that makes you feel," Dr. Anderson asked, leaning forward as if her were on to something, "to Matt?"

Drew just shook his head in disbelief. Had this guy set foot in a middle school any time this century?

"Matt knows how I feel," Drew muttered. "It's not exactly a news flash that he scares the crap out of me. That's kind of the point."

"I just wonder," Dr. Anderson said, "if sitting down with him and expressing the impact of his actions on you would…"

Drew did not even let him finish his thought.

"And just when would you propose this little heart to heart happens?" he shot back. "When Matt is shoving me into my locker, or when he's stealing my shorts when I'm changing for PE?"

It was the wrong thing to say. It made Dr. Anderson think that, but for the logistical complications, Drew was all for it. The sarcasm was entirely lost on him.

"Oh, we can make it happen," Dr. Anderson said, nodding to emphasize his point. "Matt Santoni can be asked, can be *made,* to sit with you and discuss his behavior, with adult supervision." He paused to push his glasses back up his nose. "With no lockers or gym shorts involved at all."

Drew thought he detected the slightest hint of a smile.

"I'm going to pass on that," Drew replied emphatically (*adv,* with great force or definiteness). He wanted to make it crystal clear that there was no way he was sitting down with Matt Santoni. He could not envision any way on earth—forget earth, any way in the entire galaxy – that voluntarily sitting down with Matt Santoni and letting him know, "Gee, it hurts when you whip me with your towel," or "Gosh, it's kind of embarrassing to be called *Gayboy"* or "I feel socially and physically powerless when you block my way in the hallway," would improve things one iota.

Drew spent most of his time trying to *avoid* Matt and the scores of Matt wannabes, who all seemed to relish using Drew as their target practice. He considered it a successful day if he was able to navigate his way from the bus to his classes to lunch and the rest of his classes and back home with only one or two humiliating encounters. Now if Dr. Anderson could hypnotize him into being invisible, or could help him strategize some new and clever avoidance tactics, *that* would be worth the big bucks he charged for every session.

Drew saw his mom looking at him expectantly. He hadn't even heard what she'd asked, but he knew some kind of answer, some acknowledgement of the fact that she was sitting there across from him at the kitchen table, doing her inept best to make him feel better, was warranted (*adj,* necessary).

"Good smoothie, Mom," he said, noisily slurping the last of it up the straw.

"It *is* particularly good today," Mara agreed enthusiastically.

She smiled encouragingly at her son. What was going on under those red curls of his? There was a time when he told her all about his day, in one long, stream-of-consciousness litany that was as entertaining as it was detailed. But the enthusiasm for both the days and the recounting of them had begun dwindling in middle school and now it was all she could do to pull monosyllabic answers out of him. "How was your day?" she'd ask brightly, putting a plate of steaming hot banana bread smothered in peanut butter on the table with a big glass of milk. "Okay," Drew would mumble, commenting more on the snack than on how he'd spent the last eight hours away from her. "Anything you want to talk about?" she'd ask hopefully, knowing it was rough going with some of those mean boys at school. Drew would shake his head no. "Anything you need help figuring out?" His response would be another bite of bread or a request for more milk. "You know I'm here for you, right?" she'd ask, and this time the nod would be affirmative. But no words. No details. Just one big wall of stoic silence.

She could only hope that he was more forthcoming with Dr. Anderson.

CHAPTER SIX

Scanning the room, Drew saw only one other kid. Everyone else was an adult, and many of them, especially in his division, were *old* adults. He knew this was probably not what Dr. Anderson had in mind, but a deal was a deal.

"I'm Paul," his opponent said, extending his hand. "Paul Franklin. Number 38."

Drew shook Paul's hand. "Drew Founts-Hiltone, Number 42."

Paul scrunched up his face at Drew's hyphenated last name. It was a common reaction.

"First tournament?" he asked.

Drew nodded.

"Do you know about the timer and challenges and all that?" Paul asked. "I know that was a big adjustment for me when I first started playing competitively."

"Yeah, they had an informational session for all the unrated players before registration," Drew replied. Mr. Springer had also talked him through what to expect and had played some games with him on the clock so that Drew could get used to playing with it.

"Welcome to the fifth annual Charlotte SCRABBLE Tournament," Miles Johnson said, holding a mike as he walked the perimeter of the room. "Please find your seats and your opponents. Division Four is in green over here," he pointed to the side of the room near the doors that led out to the hallway, where Drew and Paul were sitting. "Division Three is any table in blue, right over there," he motioned to the row of tables next to Drew's section. "Division Two is in yellow, right here where I'm standing and Division One is in black, way back here where no one can bother them."

Chuckles from around the room.

"The expert players are notorious babies," Paul whispered to Drew.

Mr. Springer had already warned him. "It's not a hobby for some of these folks. SCRABBLE is their *life*. They spend hours every day studying new words, they can rattle off anagrams like nobody's business, and they are all a bit, well, what you'd expect of folks who do nothing but SCRABBLE."

Drew peered over at them. They looked harmless enough. It was clear their clothes and overall appearance were not at the top of their agenda, but other than that they didn't seem particularly recognizable as word freaks. They all seemed to know each other. In fact, the entire room seemed to know each other, even though it was clear not everyone was from the Charlotte SCRABBLE circuit. Paul, for instance, was from Washington, D.C., which Drew would have known even if it wasn't printed on his nametag because of his board, which had his name and city inscribed in SCRABBLE letters around the border. That was perhaps the biggest surprise of the tournament thus far. It wasn't the fact that all these SCRABBLE enthusiasts existed and were able to fill the ballroom at the Airport Sheraton, or that the registration table was filled with flyers for upcoming tournaments all around the country, further proof that there was this whole, secret SCRABBLE world out there that met and competed in hotels just like this. (Drew wondered what other secret societies were out there that people were clueless about. Were there Bullies Anonymous meetings that Matt Santoni attended every weekend? Did the popular kids go to clandestine tutorials on how to maintain their popularity and keep the middle school scum like him in their place?) It was all a bit overwhelming.

But the biggest surprise was all the equipment and SCRABBLE paraphernalia. Who knew? The clocks were not the clunky, oversized black ones Mr. Springer borrowed from the RMS Chess Club each week. These were sleek and colorful and digital. And the tile bags came in every shape and color you could imagine, as did the tiles! There were red tiles and purple tiles and yellow tiles. Miles had explained that the tiles had to be regulation, meaning they had to be smooth and uniform. Raised print meant that you could cheat and feel which letters you were pulling out of the bag. Miles also told them they had to hold the bag up to the side of their heads when drawing tiles, so that no one could accuse them of peering inside to handpick the ones they wanted. He said you had to make sure that whoever you were sitting next to at your assigned table did not have the same color tiles as you did so that you didn't mistakenly draw from the wrong tile bag. That had apparently happened on more than one occasion. It was an awful lot to remember and Drew was getting increasingly concerned that he'd inadvertently commit a terrible SCRABBLE faux-pas (*n*, gaffe or blunder). He wondered if *faux-pas* was good. It was too late to look it up, but he found himself doing that a lot lately. "Get your tushies in the cushies," Mrs. Snyder admonished the class, and Drew wondered, "Is tushy good?" Or when he told Dr. Anderson that it was hard to be positive about school when you worried every day that you were going to get the crap beat out of you, he wondered, "Is crap good?"(*v*, to throw a 2,3, or 4 in a dice game). Drew would see a sign or billboard, like the sign for Sharon Amity Road that he passed every day on his way to school, and he would find himself anagramming the letters to form new words, imagining that those were the letters on his rack.

"Oh boy, I've created a monster," Mr. Springer said, when Drew confided that he had a dream about playing QUIZMASTER on the triple triple for 410 points.

But the most surprising of all were the boards. These made the plastic SCRABBLE boards at school, that came ten to a box in the School SCRABBLE kit Mr. Springer had ordered from the National SCRABBLE Association, look like crap (*n*, refuse, rubbish, junk, litter). These were round and sleek, mounted on turnstiles so that they swiveled effortlessly, and almost all of them were personalized. There were boards made out of granite; boards that folded up for easy transport; and boards that looked like they cost more than the Founts-Hiltone's Honda Civic

"Miles runs a really good tournament," Paul commented. "That's why I travel down for it. He always starts on time and he's really organized. He's been a director for at least 10 years and he's been playing competitive SCRABBLE for something like 30 years."

Thirty years? What on earth was Drew doing here.

"How long have you been playing?" he asked Paul with trepidation (*n*, fear or uneasiness about the future or a future event).

"Going on two years," Paul said. "I just can't seem to get my rating up. I'll have a good tournament but then a newbie like you will beat me and send my rating plummeting again."

Drew looked confused.

"Do you know how the ratings work?" Paul asked, chuckling.

"Not really. I know I'm unrated and that I won't be after this tournament, but that's about it."

"Well, it's super complicated, but basically the number of games that we're each expected to win is calculated after each tournament, and that number is subtracted from the number of games that we actually did win. Your rating is then adjusted by the product of this difference with a multiplier," Paul looked up to see if Drew was still with him, "which depends on the number of games you have played and your pre-tournament rating."

The butterflies that had begun fluttering in Drew's stomach when he'd first entered the room were flying around like crazy now. He was feeling nervous to the point of nauseated, and he felt like calling Dr. Anderson and asking, "Happy now?"

Dr. Anderson had advised Drew – and when Dr. Anderson strongly advised something, it was pretty much a direct order – to find an activity or social outlet that did not involve school. "You will hopefully get a fresh start in high school, when you can carve out a new reputation for yourself and find more like-minded kids," Dr. Anderson said one day, when Drew complained that it didn't matter how much he worked on being less sensitive and changing *his* behavior because the other part of the equation – the bullies and the kids like Evan and Scott and Matt, who made a sport out of tormenting him – were never going to see him as anything but a loser, "but for now we have to get you through middle school. And to do that I think it would be advisable for you to do something apart from Randolph Middle School. Join a club or a class in Matthews or Mint Hill, where no one knows you."

"Sounds like I'm going into the Witness Protection Program," Drew commented wryly.

"It's more like the *psyche* protection program," Dr. Anderson said. "Your ego takes a bruising every day and we need to find something for you to do away from the bullies so it can take a break from all that abuse."

Somehow, fourteen games of SCRABBLE over two days in a hotel off I-85, playing mainly adults who could give a flying leap about Drew's fragile ego because they were here to compete --- there was, after all, prize money involved and the carefully guarded ratings Paul said everyone cared so much about – was probably not what Dr. Anderson had in mind.

"Okay, it is now 9:00 and we're ready to begin. If your opponent is not at your table by 9:05, you may start his or her clock," Miles announced. "Happy tiling everyone. Bingos to all."

And with that the games were officially underway.

Drew wondered if the clock could be neutralized if he needed to throw up.

Paul went first, having drawn a B to beat Drew's M. He picked seven tiles out of the bag one at a time, slowly and deliberately placing them each face down on his score sheet. After he had drawn his seventh tile, he said, "Okay," and began looking at them as he placed them on his rack, which was Drew's sign that he could start his clock.

Drew picked H, K, O, Y, L, A and A. Before he could study his letters and rack his brain for word possibilities, Paul was placing his tiles on the board.

He put an E on the center square, then an S before it, then an A, H and P to form the word PHASE, with the P on the double letter score. Drew thought it was a waste of an S, to use it in the middle of a word rather than hooking it on to a word that was already on the board to form a plural and perhaps bingo with it, but maybe Paul knew something he didn't.

As it turns out, he did.

Because he wasn't done. He placed IN in front of PHASE to form the word INPHASE.

"Eighty," Paul announced, looking pleased with himself. He hit his clock, signaling the official end of his turn and the start of Drew's.

"Hold," Drew said, trying to read Paul's body language. He had definitely never heard of the word INPHASE before, but surely there were going to be lots of words out there that he didn't know. On the other hand, maybe Paul was taking advantage of the fact that he was an inexperienced kid playing among adults, and he figured Drew would be too intimidated to challenge.

"Okay, Dr. Anderson, this is for you," Drew thought to himself. "This is the new me. I will not be intimidated. I will stand up for myself. I will..."

"Challenge," Drew said, much more forcefully than he'd intended.

He stopped the clock, so that neither his nor Paul's time would be running while they went to the computer. Before getting up, he put his tiles face down, another thing Miles had advised the newbies to do so that your tiles weren't inadvertently seen by your opponent on the way back from challenges, and then joined Paul at one of the many computers set up around the room.

Drew, the challenger, typed in the word INPHASE.

Paul hit the tab key.

Green screen. YES, the play is ACCEPTABLE.

Drew's heart sank.

They returned to the table and Drew started Paul's clock, since it was his turn again.

Paul drew seven more tiles, and within moments, placed QI (*n,* the vital force that in Chinese thought is inherent in all things) above the I and N for 26 points.

"One hundred and six," Drew said, tallying Paul's first two scores.

Talk about discouraging. He hadn't even taken a turn yet and he was down by over one hundred points.

Drew decided to use the E in INPHASE to form the word HOKEY (*adj,* false, contrived) for 30 points.

Paul played FOGEY (*n,* an old-fashioned person) for 32 points.

Drew played FORA *(n.* a public meeting place) for 21 points.

Paul used up 4 minutes for his next play, making Drew think he was about to bingo again, but he finally played JOT for 26 points.

Score: Paul, 164 points. Drew, 51 points.

Drew had F L A T R M E on his rack. If he could dump his F and L, he'd have M A T R E left. With both blanks still out there and 3 of the 4 S's, the odds were good that he'd get a good bingo rack the next turn. Drew knew that was his only way of catching Paul. But where to dump the F and L?

I think FLO is good, Drew thought. *Isn't that like ebb and flo?*

He put the F and L above the O in JOT, with the F on the triple letter square.

"Fourteen points," he announced,

Paul didn't even hesitate or ask him to hold.

"Challenge," he said, stopping the clock.

Drew instantly regretted playing FLO. He should have played something he was sure of. It was a stupid risk to take for only 14 points, especially when he was already so far behind.

This time Paul, the challenger, typed in the word and Drew then hit the TAB key.

Red screen.

NO, the play is UNACCEPTABLE.

Ugh.

Even though Paul had seemed perfectly nice before the game, Drew felt as if Paul had suddenly joined ranks with Matt Santoni. Or, in terms of Dr. Anderson's constant query *And how did that make you feel?* Drew suddenly felt as if he'd just been punched in the stomach by Matt. Total helplessness and despair. And this was supposed to be *helping* his self-esteem? Hardly!

They returned to the board, passing by Paul's rack on the way back. He had neglected to turn over his tiles, and Drew caught a glimpse of them. He wasn't trying to cheat; his eyes just naturally gravitated in that direction and besides, Paul should have turned them over. Drew saw that Paul had a blank and A, S, T, E. He couldn't see the rest of his letters, but it was enough to fill him with dread. Very bingo-friendly letters.

He wondered again if throwing up happened on his time or if the clock would be neutralized.

Dejectedly, Drew removed his F and L from the board and recorded a 0, his second of the game, for his lost challenge on the score sheet.

Paul hooked the S that Drew had glimpsed on the end of JOT to form the word JOTS and used his blank as an R to form the word STARTER (*n,* one that starts) for 82 points.

"Two hundred and forty," Drew said, tallying Paul's score and making a supreme effort not to sound as devastated as he felt.

I am way out of my league Drew thought to himself. *So much for this building up my confidence!*

Drew played EF (*n,* the letter F) for 14 points (*"That's* what I should have played last time!" he grumbled) and then Paul played AECIA. Drew didn't hold him, even though he'd never seen that word and doubted it was good. But he'd lost his nerve.

Had he challenged, he would have lost yet again. (AECIA, *n,* a spore-producing organ of certain fungi.)

Drew pulled the second blank and bingoed with DOUBLER. The board was pretty closed off so it was all he could come up with. He would have preferred to play a word he was confident *was* a word; he couldn't even use DOUBLER in a sentence, which was usually his own litmus test for whether a word was playable or not. But given that he had 206 points to Paul's 404, he figured he had nothing to lose.

Paul did not challenge it. (DOUBLER, *n,* one that doubles; to make twice as great.)

He then played TOWIEST, hooking the S on DOUBLERS.

Drew was 0 for 2 with challenges. He knew he shouldn't challenge it. Just because a word looked funny, wrong, didn't mean it was unacceptable. Drew had learned that the hard way. But *towiest*? Come on!

"Challenge," Drew said, against his better judgment.

Off they went to the computer for their third time.

Paul appeared to be smirking. *Here we go again*, Drew thought dejectedly.

Red screen! NO, the play is UNACCEPTABLE.

Paul smiled sheepishly. "Figured it was worth a try," he said.

Drew's euphoria was short-lived.

A few turns later, Paul bingoed for a third time with COOTIES (*n, pl.,* a body louse) for 66 points.

The final score: Paul, 532. Drew, 312.

But Drew no longer felt like throwing up. It was over, and he had survived.

"Good game, " Drew said, extending his hand.

Paul seemed surprised.

"Good game," he said, smiling and shaking Drew's hand. "You did just fine for your first-ever tournament game. You're how old? Eleven? Twelve?" Drew nodded. No one ever guessed that he was *older* than he was. " You're going to be a formidable player in no time."

"That's a spread of two hundred and eleven points, right?" Drew asked, jotting down that discouraging number under the +/- column on his score sheet.

"My first tournament," Paul confided, "was a New Year's Tournament in 2005. I lost all 21 games and my spread was astronomical. Once it surpassed 1000 points, I decided I'd hang my hat on getting a spread of negative two thousand and five points to, you know, mark the new year." Drew smiled. Paul was clearly a silver lining kind of guy. "I almost made it, too," Paul added.

Drew's next opponent was a hugely overweight woman who looked older than his grandmother. She was wearing SCRABBLE tile earrings; a K in one ear and an H in the other. She was also wearing a sweatshirt that had WORD GEEK emblazoned across it, also in SCRABBLE tile letters.

"Kitty Herndon," she said. "You must be Drew."

"Nice to meet you," Drew said, sitting down. "I just lost by over 200 points so please don't beat up on me too badly."

"Oh, you're too precious to beat up on," Kitty said, laughing. "I'm a sucker for redheads."

Drew got out a new score sheet. Kitty had gone first in her first game, so that meant Drew, who went second against Paul - third, actually, if you took into account his failed challenge of INPHASE (*adj,* having matching electrical phases) - would go first in this game.

As the game got underway, Drew realized his nervousness had totally dissipated. It was as if the mammoth loss against Paul was the realization of his worst fears. He'd been totally humiliated; it was over, and he'd survived without any battle scars. There was no longer anything to fear. And knowing that, knowing that Paul, an adult, a seasoned player, had once lost all 21 games in a single tournament, knowing that Kitty had nothing but good will towards the little pipsqueaks like him, and hearing the simultaneous rattle of 50 tile bags shaking as games began all around him, well, he later told Dr. Anderson it was the happiest and most relaxed he'd felt in a really, really long time.

Drew and Kitty were neck and neck for the first six turns or so until Drew, with no power tiles on his rack, was able to play RELATING using the T in THIN on the triple triple in the upper right hand corner of the board for a whopping 131 points. He never looked back, winning the game 507 to 348, with a spread of 169. His cumulative, after the first two games, was negative 42 points. Not great, but certainly a lot more manageable than negative 211.

Besides, he'd *won.* He'd won! Against a rated player. Against an adult. And a really nice, gracious loser to boot.

"Oh, to be your age and be so smart," Kitty gushed. "I'll be reading about you in *The SCRABBLE News* in no time."

Not every opponent was as kind. Neil Chesterfield, opponent number three, was a grumpy man in his mid-thirties, with teeth that were both prominent and stained (a bad combination) and a flannel shirt that looked (and smelled!) like he'd been wearing it for several days in a row. He barely made eye contact with Drew before the game, and made a point of recounting each of Drew's plays, as if Drew would intentionally miscount his score but for Neil's evil eye vigilance.

After Drew played FAUX (*adj,* not genuine; fake) for 30 points, he was startled to hear Neil yell out "Director!" while he was in the midst of drawing his new tiles.

Miles came running up to their table and several players at adjoining tables turned to see what the commotion was about; what grave infraction of the rules had been committed.

"Yes?" Miles said, looking from Neil to Drew.

Drew's heart was racing. What did he do?

"This boy," Neil spat out the word *boy* like it was an insult, "hit his clock *while* he was saying his score, not *after* doing so."

What? Drew had no idea what Neil was talking about. He certainly hadn't done that on purpose, if he even understood what it was he had supposedly done. He once again felt like he was going to throw up, like Matt Santoni had cornered him in the boys' bathroom, the one at the far side of the 8th grade lockers, where no teachers ever ventured.

"Now Neil," Miles said, adopting the tone one uses with an unruly child, "Drew here is an unrated player who is playing in his first tournament. Let's cut him a little slack, shall we?"

"The rules are the rules," Neil growled. "If this *kid* wants to play, he's got to abide by them."

"Just be sure to hit your clock *after* you say your score," Miles said to Drew, shaking his head at Neil as he walked away.

Drew nodded, totally flustered.

Just my luck to end up facing a grown up version of Matt Santoni.

Neil played U and S following Drew's X, hooking the S on the end of MANUAL forming the words XUS and MANUALS. The S was on a double word score, meaning that both words Neil created were doubled, for a total of 40 points.

As Neil was tallying the points, which put him significantly ahead with very few tiles left in the bag *and* messing up the one spot on the board Drew could bingo, which he'd planned to do by hooking his O on the end of AD and playing the word BOOKING *(n,* an engagement), Drew suddenly remembered that XU *(n,* a monetary unit of Vietnam) does not take an S. XI takes an S, but XU does not. He learned that the hard way in a game against Mr. Springer at SCRABBLE Club a few weeks earlier.

"Challenge," Drew said, after Neil had hit his clock.

Drew could tell immediately, from Neil's expression that registered first shock that *the kid* had challenged him and then annoyance that he'd been busted, that Neil had known it was a phony when he'd played it. He hadn't counted on Drew knowing that, though. And Drew wouldn't put it past him to have created the scene with the director to flummox him so that he wouldn't challenge even if he had been inclined to do so.

The play was unacceptable. Drew tried hard not to smirk on his way back to the table. It took even more effort to keep from grinning, or doing his best imitation of Nelson Munz on the Simpsons, saying *Ha-a-a-aha-a-a-a-a*, all drawn out and obnoxious, when he proceeded to follow up the challenge with BOOKING for 86 points.

Drew ended the tournament with a 2-12 record.

He wasn't expected to win any games, given that he was unrated, so two was actually not bad. Especially considering that one of those victories was against Neil. He didn't win a single other game after that, but Drew didn't care. In fact, he wouldn't want it any other way.

Beating Neil was sweet vengeance, not just on Neil, Player Number 31 in Division 4 at the Charlotte SCRABBLE Invitational, but on all the Neils out there who tormented him. "Take that," Drew thought, as he wrote his name under Winner on the results slip and Neil's under Loser.

He knew Dr. Anderson would read all sorts of stuff into that. Yeah, yeah, I'm a winner and the mean bully is a loser. Whatever. But secretly, Drew had to admit that seeing it in writing made it somehow official and significant. And he had to admit, maybe not to Dr. Anderson but certainly to himself, that it felt good. Really good.

CHAPTER SEVEN

"How about beau?" Elliot asked. "It'd be a good vowel dump."

"And that's a pretty good leave," Lily agreed, referring to the letters left on their rack and trying not to look at her mom, settled among the cushions on the couch, at the mention of the word beau (*n,* boyfriend). "We might even be able to beat this guy for once."

Jeremy smiled while shuffling his tiles. "Two against one, it's two against one," he said, while placing an X at the end of beau to form beaux (*n, pl,* boyfriend) and EXHUMED (*v,* to dig up). "Seventy-eight plus fifty is one hundred and twenty-eight."

Elliot looked at Lily, his mouth open in astonishment.

"I know," she said, laughing. "I told you."

"You said good," Elliot agreed, "not *one hundred and twenty-eight points on your first turn* good!"

"Two against one," Jeremy said again, adding, "Two against one."

They had tried playing three-way, the first time Elliott came over for dinner, but that hadn't worked at all. It was too big a change. Three players meant no clock, since it was only designed for two players. And three players messed up the routine. "Not your turn!" Jeremy barked, when Elliott tried to play after Lily, "Not your turn!" Jeremy became so agitated that Elliot quickly agreed to simply sit back and watch, but he offered Lily tips and suggestions until they'd eased into playing together, as a team, in the two against one format Jeremy not only tolerated, but enjoyed.

"It's two against one," Jeremy said again, "One hundred and thirty for me and twelve for you two."

"Rub it in, why don't you?" Elliot said, sighing.

"Hey, now you know how I feel every week," Lily agreed, smiling. But actually, he didn't. He couldn't know that playing with him, as a team, was nothing like what she usually felt.

She conjured up a mental calendar, counting backwards to the day she'd first met Elliott Springer, and it was hard to believe that it had only been four weeks. Four weeks that sped by, because she could still feel the panic and desperation on the day of the accident as if it had just happened yesterday, but weeks that had also crawled by in that it seemed like she'd known Elliott much longer than that, especially considering how unusually comfortable Jeremy was with the new addition to their home and routine.

And her mom couldn't even claim to know Elliot *that* long, because Lily had to fast forward another six days in her mental calendar to mark the day Eliot and her mom officially met. Those first few days, she was too out of it to even register Lily, her own child. "It's the meds," Doctor Slatery explained, after sitting Lily down on the ugly plastic couch outside the emergency room, where Elliot had driven her as soon as they'd heard the news. Dr. Slatery calmly informed her that her mother had broken her left femur and had a compound fracture of her left arm. "She'll be pretty out of it for a few days," he said, "so we'll keep her here so that we can keep an eye on her."

And while Charlotte Presybeterian kept an eye on Sally, Elliot kept an eye on her kids. Not officially, and not all the time – that task fell to Aunt Nicole, who was on a plane within hours of Lily's call, and who stayed with them for a full ten days after Sally came home, filling the freezer with casseroles and leaving only because Sally insisted that if she didn't, Sally would drive her to the airport herself, cast and all. "You have kids of your own who need you," Sally insisted, when Nicole protested that there was no way she could leave her so incapacitated (*adj,* debilitated). "And a husband too." They both knew that cut both ways, since Mike, Nicole's husband, was no doubt missing her but was also able to pick up the slack while she was away, something Sally did not have in her life, and hadn't had for a good long time.

But what Sally did have, and this reassured Nicole enough to finally leave, albeit with promises to hop back in a jiffy at the merest hint of being needed again, was Elliot. By the time Sally met him, when he came by with Chinese food on her third night home, the other members of her family felt as if they'd known him forever, or at least for much longer than they'd actually known him. And if Sally had any misgivings about playing catch up in getting to know a man who already seemed so at ease and familiar with her two children, it was that fact that actually eased her mind. For Jeremy to accept a stranger into their midst, albeit with a few hiccups, like the ill-fated three-way SCRABBLE game, did more to give Elliot the protective mama bear seal of approval than just about anything short of a thorough background check could have done. Even Lily, usually so guarded and protective of Jeremy, would grin with unabashed delight to report that Elliott was on his way over or that he had just called to see if they needed anything.

"So is he cute?" Samantha asked, when Lily reported that Elliot was coming over that evening.

"Or is it hard to tell under all that armour?" Jessie teased.

The three girls, best friends since the second grade, when they'd all banded together to insist on being included in the boys' kickball game at recess, had dubbed Elliott Lily's Knight in Shining Armor after he'd swooped in to save her the night of her mom's accident.

"He is pretty cute," Lily said, "In a non movie-star kind of way. He's not old like Mr. Furman, and he certainly dresses better (rumor had it hat Mr. Furman owned only two pairs of pants --- both horribly out of style – and he simply rotated them in and out of his closet until he did the laundry every weekend) but you can also tell it's not his first year of teaching. He doesn't look like he just graduated from college yesterday, the way Mr. Pierce does." Half of the 8th grade girls had a humongous crush on Mr. Pierce, with his buzz cut and dimpled smile, but Lily didn't share their infatuation. "If I were you, I'd try to set your mom up with Mr. Pierce," Stephanie Darius suggested to Lily one day. "You're so lucky that she's single and available." Lily just rolled her eyes. She had no desire to set her mom up with Mr. Pierce, or with anyone else, for that matter. She wanted her mom to be happy, but she also knew they had a good, insular unit; a routine that worked, and she was reluctant to mess with it in any way.

So why was she okay with Elliott's sudden and almost immediate inclusion in her tight little family unit, about which she was ordinarily so protective?

"I think it's because he saved you," Samantha surmised (v, to conclude that something is the case on the basis of only limited evidence or intuitive feeling) when they were discussing Elliot during lunch.

"Yeah," Jessie agreed, licking the egg salad that was escaping from her sandwich. Lily and Samantha watched her with disgust, shaking their heads. Jessie was the only person in the entire school who actually *liked* Crestdale's egg salad sandwiches. "Saviors get an automatic pass. They're in. You can't dislike them."

"But there's really nothing to dislike," Lily said, feeling like she had to defend Elliott. He was likable on his own merits, not just because she was transferring feelings of gratitude and relief onto him for how he'd come through for them that horrible night they'd met. He'd helped Lily keep Jeremy calm, and by remaining so calm and reassuring himself, he'd made Lily feel exactly what she was trying to convey to her bewildered brother. That everything would be okay. That it would all soon return to normal.

Samantha and Jessie laughed.

"My point exactly," Jessie said, winking at Samantha.

"No really," Lily continued, knowing her friends were teasing her but feeling nonetheless like she had to explain why Elliot got a pass, why not only Lily, but Jeremy, too, had so seamlessly accepted him into their tight little group. "He's so great the way he doesn't talk down to Jeremy. But he also gets that he's different. I don't feel like I have to explain stuff to him or apologize for why Jeremy is, you know, pulling a Jeremy."

Samantha and Jessie both knew. They had plenty of experience being over at the Mallovaris' when Jeremy was being Jeremy.

"But aren't you, you know, worried that he and your mom might hook up?" Samantha asked. She knew, thanks to late night conversations during sleepovers, when you mumble what you really think and feel, in that honesty that stems from being cocooned in darkness and two blinks away from slumber, that as much as Lily wanted her mom to be happy, she didn't want her bringing somebody new into the picture.

"I think," Lily said, realizing she meant it as she said it, "that I'd be okay with Elliott. I'd like that, actually."

It was Jessie who figured it out.

"It's because he's not some guy your mom met through a personal ad or while she was shopping at Harris Teeter," Jessie said, licking her fingers now that her sandwich was gone. "*You* found this guy. Elliot is *yours*."

Both Jessie and Samantha knew that Jeremy was not the only member of the Mallovari family who liked to be in control. They had defended their smart and pretty friend to other girls all through elementary school and middle school, girls who complained that Lily was stuck up and standoffish. But they knew better. Lily was the most generous and loyal friend you could have, and whatever standoffishness she emanated (*v,* to emit, send out, or give out) was really just her protectiveness, borne from years of serving as her brother's buffer to the outside world. Besides, boys always had crushes on Lily, from Jonas Mitchell sending her notes about how pretty she was in the second grade to Michael Fletcher relentlessly asking her out on dates all through 7th grade. Samantha and Jessie, who could see it all from their vantage point as outside observers of both the lovesick boys and the reaction of the other girls, the ones who thought they deserved the boys' attention instead of Lily, knew that most of the disdain for Lily stemmed from jealousy. Lily had those natural and effortless good looks that one either admired or resented, and her disdain for what other people thought of her (fueled, again, from the thick skin she'd developed on Jeremy's behalf) was easily misinterpreted as superiority and condescension (*n,* behavior or an example of behavior that implies that somebody is graciously lowering himself or herself to the level of people less important or intelligent).

The one flaw Lily's friends would confess she had, if pressed to pick one, was her need to be in control. They knew why and understood it for what it was, and, in fact, often teased Lily about it and good-naturedly took it into account when making plans. Like everything else in Lily's life, it had to do with her brother. Having helplessly watched Jeremy implode when Jeopardy was delayed by a technological glitch one too many times, Lily valued timeliness and order and sticking to a schedule much more than most kids her age. And certainly more than Jessie and Samantha did, which is why they had no problem letting Lily pick which night they'd go to the movies or whose house they'd assemble at to do their science project. And Lily was very selective about who could join them, which they again understood as a precaution against someone inadvertently making life more difficult than it had to be.

So it made sense that anyone who was going to make it into the Sally Mallovari dating pool would have to first get a thumbs up from Lily. And the fact that Lily had met Elliott first, and that he had passed the Jeremy test and been vetted (*v,* to subject somebody or something to a careful examination or scrutiny, especially when this involves determining suitability for something) in the most stressful of situations before he even met Sally, well, that pretty much propelled him past the usual blockades Lily put up in front of her tightly guarded family unit. Even though she hadn't thought of him as a potential suitor for her mother when she'd first met him, or even those first few times he had checked on her and Jeremy and otherwise made himself useful, the fact that she had picked him out and let him in, bit by bit, allowed her to now wholeheartedly endorse him as someone more than just the guy they met at the track.

"Eighteen," Jeremy said, placing his final four tiles, I,S, T, and A after BAR to form the word barista (*n,* one who serves coffee to the public). "And out."

"You get, um, 12 from us," Lily announced, adding up the value of the tiles left on her rack and doubling them.

"And you," Elliott said, turning to Sally, who was watching from her perch of pillows on the couch, "get a cup of coffee, if you want one. Barista made me think of Starbucks, and I'm craving a mocha frappuccino."

"Oh, that sounds awesome," Sally said. "Although you'd better make mine no whip, given that my daily walks have been put on hold."

"I'll take mine with whip, please," Lily said. "I'll come with you if you want."

"No, you will not," Sally announced from the couch, trying to sound authoritative despite being immobilized and tucked under an afghan (*n,* a woolen blanket or shawl). "You will march right off to bed. It's late and you have school tomorrow."

"Besides," Jeremy said, "you have to clean up. Loser cleans up."

"What about Elliot?" Lily asked, only pretending to be mad. "He lost too!"

"Lose*rs* clean up," Jeremy corrected himself, emphasizing the last syllable. "You're right, Lily. Lose*rs.*"

"Thanks a bunch," Elliot muttered, swatting Lily on the arm with the tile rack in mock indignation (*n,* anger or annoyance because somebody or something seems unfair or unreasonable). "I had a clean getaway all ready to go until you sold me out."

"Those are the breaks," Lily said, winking at her mom. "If I don't get coffee, I don't see why I should be helping you get out the door on your little coffee run so that you and Mom get to have a little Starbucks party without me."

As soon as she said it, she regretted it. The awkwardness that suddenly hung there, between them, meant that all three had just realized that despite the many nights Elliott had joined them for dinner since the accident, and the fact that they were all three so used to having him around, this marked the first time he and Sally would be alone together, without either Jeremy or Lily to serve as buffers.

"You know, what was I thinking?" Sally said, filling the silence. "You have school tomorrow too. You certainly don't need to be schlepping back here with Starbucks for me. I don't need the calories, anyway."

"I want to," Elliott said quietly. "Really, it's no bother."

"Well, g'night," Lily said, pecking him on the cheek.

"Good night, Lily," Elliott said, heading for the door, unsure whether to stay or leave. He turned back, his hand on the doorknob. "Let's have our goal for next time be getting within 200 points of your brother. I think that's doable, don't you?"

"Only if you study," Lily said, laughing. "I'm tired of carrying this team."

She put the SCRABBLE board away, then walked over to the couch and bent down to kiss her mother goodnight.

"Let him," she whispered into her mother's ear.

CHAPTER EIGHT

"It's no fair that Aidan and Drew are a pair," David complained. "They're by far the best players. You should split them up."

"I don't even get why you have to play in pairs, anyway," Mohammed piped up. "It's an individual game. We should play by ourselves."

"Well, that's not an option," Mr. Springer said, in a tone that let the assembled members of the Randolph Middle School SCRABBLE Club know that the gripe session was at an end. "I didn't come up with the rules, so it's pointless to argue them with me."

He looked around the room. Even though the pairs had only been established the week before, those who were happy with their assignments were sitting or standing together. Cecelia and Jennifer were perched side by side next to the computer, where they had just checked *quixotic* on Zyzzyva and confirmed that it's a word (*adj,* extremely idealistic). Not likely they'd ever be able to play it, since it didn't have any good hooks within it, but like most of the SCRABBLE Club members, they had developed an insatiable (*adj,* always needing more and impossible to satisfy) curiosity about words, voraciously (*adv,* with an insatiable appetite) reading dictionaries and word lists to learn new ones and then testing if they could be anagrammed into yet more words. Drew and Aidan were doing the same thing at the computer next to Cecelia and Jennifer, each trying to surpass each other with words they'd found during the week. Aidan was particularly fond of long words, the longer the better, like heartlessnesses and capitalizations, words he'd probably never be able to use in a game but with the right combination of letters already on the board and a huge dose of luck, he could foreseeably (*adv,* seeing or knowing beforehand) use across a triple triple for a gargantuan (*adj,* of immense size or volume; colossal) amount of points. Drew's personal favorites, which he'd discovered when simply fooling around on Zyzyvva last week when his class was in Media and he had finished the research assignment on Zambia before everyone else, were AARGH, AARRGH AND AARRGHH, all good. Very apt for how he often felt in the hallowed halls of RMS.

David and Mohammed, having lost handily to Drew and Aidan in their first game and then lost again, by a smaller margin but nonetheless a definitive loss, in their match against Jennifer and Cecelia, were itching for a change of partners. Each was convinced his partner was at fault for the pair's less than stellar performance, but Mr. Springer didn't seem at all sympathetic to their plight.

"Look at Brandon and Lucy," he said. "You don't see them complaining, do you?"

Brandon, who had developed a crush on Lucy and wanted nothing more than to be near her and spend time with her, would only have complained if he *hadn't* been partnered with her. He couldn't quite believe his luck. But in an effort to act cool and nonchalant, because the last thing on earth he wanted to do was to let her know that's how he felt, he shrugged his shoulders and rolled his eyes, as if to say that he, at least, was accepting the fact that there was nothing to be done about the pairings.

"So don't forget to take home these permission slips," Mr. Springer reminded the group. "This is not your typical school club outing. We're talking about flying to Rhode Island, missing school, and a considerable cost, so it's important your parents understand everything that's involved."

David's eyes grew big when he saw the total that was needed for each student to be able to go to the National School SCRABBLE tournament. "No way my mom can afford this," he said.

"Yeah, why can't the school pay for us to go?" Mohammed piped up.

Elliott Springer was well aware that the trip would be too costly for several of the players. "I'm working on getting some scholarship money together," he announced. "And any ideas *you* guys can come up with for helping fund the trip, bring them on." Looking around the room, especially at the kids like David and Marcus who had never played SCRABBLE before and had probably never left North Carolina, Elliott fervently hoped he'd be able to come up with some creative funding. He really wanted them to have this opportunity. The sports teams had a booster club and all sorts of school support, but there was nothing established for the SCRABBLE-playing members of

RMS. "I didn't even know there was such a thing," Mrs. Villroy said when Elliott approached her with the idea of taking several teams to Rhode Island.

The kids were particularly pumped because Mr. Springer had asked Drew to talk them through his experience playing in the Charlotte tournament. The rest of the club listened with rapt attention, appreciating the fact that he was the only one who had left the security of the club and tested the waters of actual competition, with *adults* no less. They devoured the score sheets he brought back, asked him questions about the players and the rules and highlights of his games, and cheered loudly when he described his game with the odious Neil. Drew had taken on a sort of Assistant Coach position, one he'd assumed reluctantly at first but had come to enjoy. He was not accustomed to being in charge; to having others look to him to see what to do or what he thought. In fact, the last time he'd been shown the respect and awe reserved for him at SCRABBLE Club had been in kindergarten. It felt pretty good, although it was usually pretty short-lived. As soon as he left SCRABBLE Club and headed to his first block class, where Matt Santoni greeted him with "Hey Founts-Hiltone, how's your boyfriend?" or Joe Fletcher nabbed his backpack and ran off down the hall with it, Drew's social status and confidence plummeted down to where it belonged.

"It could be that everyone who wants to go will not be able to go," Mr. Springer warned them. "But I've paid – or rather, RMS has, so be sure to thank Mrs. Villroy, for five teams to represent us at the tournament, so there are spots for all of you." Cheers and fists in the air. "We now have to work on getting there," Mr. Springer added.

"Will we room with our partners?" Jennifer asked, which made Brandon's heart race until he saw Lucy's expression, on which disgust and panic were both evident. She needn't have worried.

"The Providence Biltmore is a pricey hotel, so we'll probably be four to a room," Mr. Springer replied. "And of course the girls will be with the girls and the boys with the boys."

Lucy was not the only girl who looked relieved.

"How about a bake sale?" Aidan suggested. "My mom makes awesome heathbar brownies we could sell."

"Yeah, that'll like, pay, for *one* of us to go, and probably not even that," David said dejectedly. Even though he wanted a new partner, like Drew, with whom he'd be sure to win or at least do really, really well, he would go with anyone at all if he could just go. He'd gone to Atlanta two years ago for his cousin's wedding, and he'd crossed the line into South Carolina a few times, but that was it. To actually get on a plane and fly someplace, and stay in a nice hotel, and see a different part of the country... it all sounded awesome, and frustratingly out of his reach.

"A bake sale is a good start," Mr. Springer said, smiling at Aidan, "but I was thinking more about asking businesses and organizations to sponsor us. Any thoughts," he asked, turning back to the entire group, "on whom we could hit up?"

Cecelia raised her hand.

"How about a bookstore?" she suggested, quietly. "They like words."

"Excellent," Mr. Springer said, writing *Bookstore* on the dry erase board followed by *Barnes & Noble, Joseph-Beth Booksellers, Borders* and *Little Professor Book Store.*

"Any other ideas?"

"How about Target or Walmart?" Drew suggested. "I have seen letters from schools thanking them up on their walls near Customer Service, so they must give out money."

"Great," Mr. Springer said, adding them to the list on the board.

"And doesn't Harris Teeter already give our school money, like a cash back kind of thing for using our VIC cards?" Lucy asked.

Her answer was the fact that Mr. Springer added Harris Teeter to the list.

"Now," Mr. Springer said, scanning the group, "I want each of you to take on one of these stores as your responsibility."

"What does that mean?" David asked, not liking the sound of it.

"It means," Mr. Springer explained, "that you are to find out if, say, Target does in fact give scholarship money or grants for things like this."

"Oh, that's easy," David said. "There's a Harris Teeter right up the street from me. I'll take them."

"*And,*" Mr. Springer continued, "once you have figured out that they do and in what form the request must be made – a letter or an application or meeting with a customer service representative – you are responsible for making sure that gets done."

A chorus of groans, some accompanied by looks of incredulity (*n*, a state of feeling or disbelief), followed his announcement.

"And did I mention this all has to happen before we meet next week?" Mr. Springer asked.

"What? Why?" Mark protested. "The tournament is not until April."

"Yes, but these things can take lots of time and we need to know what kind of money we have to play with so we can plan accordingly," Mr. Springer replied. "So divvy up who's doing what and I want full reports on your progress next week."

"If we bring in the money" David asked, "do we get to keep it?"

"No, it'll go into the SCRABBLE Club account, to be doled out as needed."

Mr. Springer noted that David still saw his ability to go to the tournament as a total long shot. He waited until David looked up and he winked at him. "You have my personal guarantee that everyone who wants to go and has his or her parents' permission *will* go. We will find a way."

"Whatever," David said, shrugging his shoulders to indicate he didn't care.

He didn't fool anyone.

CHAPTER NINE

"So who wants to join Drew in the ranks of seasoned SCRABBLE players?" Mr. Springer asked the group.

His response was a bunch of scrunched up faces, the middle-school version of "Huh?"

"I'm heading to a tournament in Raleigh next weekend," Mr. Springer explained, "and I'm taking an 8th grader from Crestdale."

"*Crestdale?*" David interrupted him. "Why?"

Mr. Springer's cheeks got a little redder. "She's, um, a family friend," he said, then quickly added, "The point is, I can fit an additional three of you in my car, so if anyone else wants to come along and get some tournament practice before the National School SCRABBLE Tournament, I'd be happy to take you."

Drew, the one player who didn't need to get his feet wet, having done so already at the Charlotte Tournament, was the only one who took Mr. Springer up on his offer. Aidan wanted to, but he had to spend the weekend with his dad. "Stupid divorce," Aidan said. "Having your parents fight over you sucks."

"What about Providence?" Drew asked with trepidation. Now that everyone was partnered up, he would be unable to play if Aidan couldn't go.

" I've already cleared that weekend with both of them," Aidan reassured him. "I told them that custody arrangement or not, that weekend is off limits."

So it was just Drew, Lily and Mr. Springer. En route to her house to pick her up, Drew asked Mr. Springer, "So who is this girl?"

"She's a friend of mine," Mr. Springer said, in between bites of the pumpkin bread Drew's mom had packed for the journey. "I met her on one of my runs earlier this year."

When they pulled in to pick Lily up, it was clear Mr. Springer was friendly with not just Lily, but her entire family. He ran in to use the bathroom and fill up his coffee thermos and when they left, Lily's mom had just as big a hug for Mr. Springer as she did for her own daughter. It was also clear that Lily was very comfortable with Mr. Springer. For one thing, she called him Elliott. And when he said, after introducing her to Drew, that it was best to let her sit up front so that she didn't throw up all over them since she had a propensity (*n,* a tendency to demonstrate particular behavior) for carsickness, she punched him in the arm.

Rather than feeling envious or resentful of the close relationship Lily obviously enjoyed with his beloved teacher, Drew instead enjoyed being lumped right in with them. It was as if the negativity of his social struggles at Randolph and the inherent awkwardness of seeing one's teacher outside of school dissipated as soon as Lily joined them. Her easy banter (*n,* lighthearted teasing or amusing remarks that are exchanged between people) and the way she looked Drew directly in the eyes when talking to him and treated him like he was on the same social footing, even if it was just for that weekend or even just that car ride, made Drew feel like he was instantly transformed into a different kid. It was as if Lily, with her easy charm and confidence, which she then bestowed on Drew as if he deserved it, as if there was no question as to his being equally cool and worthy of being acknowledged by someone like her, elevated him into the kind of kid he wished he could be instead of the kind of loser nerd he was.

Drew found himself wishing fervently *(adv,* with great warmth or intensity) that Lily went to Randolph instead of Crestdale. If someone like Lily gave him the time of day at Randolph, he'd have it made. But it was enough to simply enjoy her company, and marvel at the fact that she appeared to be enjoying his, at least for the weekend, this oasis away from the ego-pummeling ridicule he endured during the week.

"So what do you think?" Mr. Springer asked, turning around and facing Drew in the backseat when they'd stopped for gas and Lily had not yet returned from the restroom. "She's a pretty great kid, huh?"

"Mmm hmmm," Drew said. Despite his incredibly advanced vocabulary and his SCRABBLE prowess, he could come up with no better adjectives. "She sure is," he agreed.

On the ride to Raleigh, Drew and Mr. Springer filled Lily in on what to expect and reassured her that it would be okay. Lily, in return, gave Drew some great SCRABBLE tips, like Betsy's Foot (all the letters that can be added to KA to make new, three-letter words) and other fun mnemonics (*n,* a device to assist the memory) that she'd learned from her big brother. Drew's personal favorite was Knight Swam, which was a mnemonic for all of the letters that work in front of AE. He conjured up a mental image of a knight, in full armor, swimming in a moat full of AEs.

"You can try to memorize KAE (*n,* a bird resembling a crow); NAE (*adv,* no; not); GAE (*v,* to go, to move along); HAE (*v,* to have; to be in possession of); TAE (*prep,* to; in the direction of); SAE (*adv,* so); WAE (*n,* woe, tremendous grief); and MAE (*n,* more, a greater amount)," Lily said, reading the words off the SCRABBLE Cheat Sheet Jeremy had made for her, "or," she grinned, folding the paper up, "you can just remember KNIGHT SWAM."

"That is so cool," Drew gushed, knowing that he'd picture a knight swimming every time he saw AE on the board or on his rack from now on. "Thanks!"

"Don't thank me," Lily replied. "Thank Jeremy. He came up with it."

"Not that *he* needs mnemonics," Elliot noted, winking at Lily.

"Why isn't he coming with us?" Drew asked.

Lily and Mr. Springer looked at each other.

"He's a really good player," Lily said, somewhat gruffly.

"Good doesn't even begin to cover it," Mr. Springer interjected.

"But, well, he can't really handle playing in a tournament." Lily looked out the window, indicating the conversation was over as far as she was concerned.

"I didn't think I'd be able to either," Drew confessed, "but it's far more intimidating in theory than in reality."

Lily continued to look out the window.

"You should talk him into coming to the next tournament," Drew persisted.

"Uh no," Lily said, shaking her head emphatically (*adv,* with great force or definiteness). "It's the *reality* that Jeremy can't deal with. Trust me."

"How come?" Drew asked. It seemed to him it was worth a try. After all, he was Lily's *older* brother. Drew had seen him standing in the doorway when they'd swung by to pick Lily up that morning. If *she* could do it, surely *he* could, especially if he was such a good player.

"He's autistic," Lily said, matter-of-factly.

Drew nodded, not really sure what that meant.

"Do you know what that is?" Lily asked, after a moment of uncomfortable silence, during which Drew racked his brain for what autism entailed.

"I think so," Drew said, nodding. "It's kind of like retarded, right?" He wondered how it was that her brother was such a good SCRABBLE player in that case.

"No, it's not like retarded at all," Lily corrected him, her tone clipped. She folded her arms and went back to looking out the window, putting an abrupt end to the camaraderie Drew thought they were all enjoying.

Mr. Springer caught Drew's eye in the rearview mirror and Drew could tell from his expression too that he'd said the wrong thing.

He was always saying the wrong thing. If it wasn't on a test, count on Drew Founts-Hiltone to botch it.

Book smarts, no problem. Top of the clsss.

Social smarts? Zilch.

"It doesn't really work that way," Dr. Anderson said, when Drew confessed, after a particularly painful evening at the Jewish Community Center, during a Jammin' at the J party his mom had begged him to attend, thinking it would be a safer social outlet than school-sponsored stuff but where he'd felt like even more of a social pariah than he did at Randolph, that he wished he could take some of his intellectual prowess and move it over to the kind of smarts he needed much more. He'd trade in his stellar grades and honor roll and academic honors any day for just a little bit of social status. He didn't even need to be one of the popular kids; he'd settle for being invisible or in the middle of the pack. Anything other than the one everyone picked on; the one who seemed like he would forever be branded a loser.

"I didn't mean it in a bad way," Drew finally said, after an uncomfortably long silence, especially coming, as it did, after the surprisingly easy and relaxed conversation they'd been enjoying up until that point. Girls his age, who were even more petty and unforgiving than the boys in his class, made Drew feel even more tongue-tied and awkward than he usually did among his peers. And that was saying something, considering his normal pond scum status. But Lily was different. She was really pretty, in a really natural and not-too-much-purple-eyeshadow-and-mascara sort of way, and she was confident. Drew was sure she was among the popular kids at her school. She had to be, because if *she* wasn't popular and cool, he couldn't imagine who *was*! But she had none of the snobbishness or condescension of the popular girls at Randolph. As soon as she emerged from her house and flung her purple duffle bag in the back of Mr. Springer's car, she acted as if they were already friends. As if they'd been hanging out together and this trip was something they'd planned on doing for a while, instead of something that had come together as it did, quickly and out of the blue.

But now he'd gone and blown it with his bone-headed comment about autism.

"I'm sorry," Lily said, turning back from the front passenger seat to look at him directly, so that he could see that she was genuinely contrite (*adj,* genuinely and deeply sorry about something). "I am super sensitive about my brother and I, um, overreact sometimes."

Drew was so relieved she wasn't mad at him he felt close to tears.

"I guess I really don't know what autism is, though," he finally managed to say. "So can you fill me in?"

"Absolutely." Lily said, glad for the opportunity to clear the air.

"Autism is a brain development disorder," she explained. "Jeremy was born with it but my mom didn't know for sure he had it until he was three."

Lily sighed. There was no way to quickly summarize Jeremy. How could she capture, for someone who had never met him, his frustrating limitations and what made him so unique; how he was so simultaneously brilliant and slow; and the fact that having him for a brother was both a joy and a burden. "Autism basically impairs his social interaction and communication," Lily continued, "which means he can't really deal in most social situations."

"Neither can I," Drew thought to himself.

"Autism causes repetitive behavior," Lily continued, again feeling that she wasn't even beginning to do justice to the complexities of Jeremy's condition. "So Jeremy has to do a lot of things a certain way and he, well, he kind of freaks out if it's not done right."

"Kind of like someone who has to count to seventeen before he can take a sip of a drink?" Drew asked. "I read about that last year. It's called obsessive compulsiveness or something like that."

"Yeah, it's kind of like that," Lily agreed. "But that only helps explain that part of the autism. The repetition, and his ability to remember things, and do them over and over again, also makes him freakishly good at stuff, like SCRABBLE."

"He's really, really smart," Mr. Springer threw in.

"Most people don't realize that," Lily agreed, nodding with appreciation.

"I'd love to meet him sometime," Drew said, "and maybe play a game of SCRABBLE with him."

"That'd be great," Lily replied, and by her smile he could tell that she meant it.

For once, Drew had actually come up with the right thing to say.

Having Lily and Mr. Springer along made the tournament so much more enjoyable. It was no longer a do-as-Dr.-Anderson suggests kind of activity, but something he genuinely and intrinsically (*adv, inherently*) enjoyed. And both the highs and lows were that much more meaningful when there was someone there experiencing them with you. As much as his parents peppered him with questions after the Raleigh tournament, there was a certain point at which their eyes glazed over because you had to be there, in the thick of it, to really get it. And now Lily and Mr. Springer got it. They were all in it together. The highlight, for Drew, was Lily's game with the odious Neil. Because to truly appreciate how insidious (*adj,* sinister) Neil Chesterfield was, you had to meet him in person. Better yet, you had to face him across a SCRABBLE board.

"I know you think you just played *saltier*," Neil sneered as he and Lily got up to head to the computer. "But you didn't. You misplaced the *e* and the *r*."

His smug smile revealed his nasty teeth, which were every bit as bad as Drew had described them. In fact, everything about Neil, from his obvious annoyance at having to play another newbie, and a *kid* at that, to his complete lack of social skills (he didn't even look up when Lily extended her hand and introduced herself) to his utter confidence in his inevitable victory, was exactly as Drew had described. Lily tried to keep her face blank and expressionless, but she was having a hard time hiding her grin. The fact that she was about to win the challenge was rendered that much more delicious by the odious Neil's conceit and presumption that *he* would win it.

Lily kept her expression noncommittal as Neil typed the word in to Zyzzvya, but inside she was dancing a happy dance and thanking Jeremy for his phenomenal word recall. He had gotten her on this very word a few weeks earlier, and Elliott had pointed out that it would be good to remember – instead of playing the safe and sure *saltier* --- because it would likely draw the challenge, just as it had with her. And there is no one she would rather have caught in her trap than Neil.

At Neil's prodding, Lily hit tab.

Green screen. THE PLAY IS ACCEPTABLE.

"What?" Neil said. His bushy eyebrows shot up in outrage.

"Shhh," a player near the computer hissed, her finger to her lips.

"Oh, bite me," Neil replied, which drew even more stares and shushes.

Lily started heading back to their board, ahead of Neil so that she didn't have to hide her grin, but he grabbed her arm.

"I must have typed it in wrong," he said, pulling her back to the computer. "I'm going to do it again."

Lily was pretty sure he wasn't allowed to do that. He was, after all, the one who had typed in the word he was challenging in the first place. But feeling certain it would yield the same result, Lily just nodded.

Neil laboriously typed the word in again, S A L T I R E (*n,* one of the basic designs used on coats of arms consisting of a diagonal cross), hitting each key slowly and deliberately. He then rechecked it against the challenge slip he'd brought with him, something he'd failed to do when he'd cockily typed it in the first time, and hit tab (something Lily, as the one being challenged, was supposed to do, but again she let it go. It wasn't going to make a difference).

Again the green screen. THE PLAY IS ACCEPTABLE.

Lily didn't even wait to see Neil's look of dumbfounded shock. She returned to her seat and tallied her score.

"I can't wait to tell Drew," she thought to herself. "He will be so psyched." She figured that even if she didn't beat Neil, the challenge going her way was victory enough.

But Lily did end up beating Neil, something both Drew and Elliott toasted at lunch.

"I can't believe he typed the word in again," Drew said, still grinning at Lily's account of her game with Neil. "Is that allowed?"

"Nope," Elliott said. "But I notice our Mister Neil Chesterfield isn't so concerned about the rules when he can skirt them to *his* benefit."

"Yeah, I thought he was such a stickler for how it's supposed to be done," Lily said.

"But now we've both beaten him," Drew mused, raising his glass. "Here's to the SCRABBLE newbies taking down the SCRABBLE meanies."

Lily and Elliott raised their glasses of sweet tea.

"Hear, hear!" they said.

CHAPTER TEN

"I think you're kind of overdoing it, Mom," Drew said, somewhat embarrassed at his mom's offerings. "It makes it look like we never get invited out and we're, well, kind of desperate."

"Nonsense," Mara Founts-Hiltone said. "You know I never go anywhere empty-handed. And no one's complained yet about my zucchini bread *or* my spiced nuts."

"That's great, Mom, but do one or the other. With the wine *and* the flowers on top of it all, it's just too much."

"There's no such thing as too much," Sam Founts-Hiltone said, popping a few nuts in his mouth before Mara slapped his hand and sealed the jar, "when it comes to your mom's cooking."

"Just relax, hon," Mara said, sensing how tense Drew was about the evening.

"Yeah, we'll try extra hard not to embarrass you," Sam said, winking at his wife.

Drew was grateful to be invited to dinner at Lily's house, and it was awfully kind of Lily's mom to include his parents too, but he didn't want it to seem like this was the first time they'd done something socially with Drew as the impetus (*n,* something that provides energy or motivation to accomplish something or to undertake something) for the invitation. Forget the fact that it *was* the first time, at a *girl's*, no less (and a really pretty one at that!); they didn't have to make that so abundantly clear.

"Sweetie, don't be so concerned about how you come across," Mara gently admonished her son. "Just be yourself."

"Yeah, 'cause that's worked so well for me up until now," Drew muttered. But he didn't want to risk another *You can overcome the bullies because you are better than they are* pep talk on the ride over or, even worse, a psychoanalysis session about why someone as fabulous as Mara Founts-Hiltone's son could be so down on himself, so he smiled and offered to carry the nuts and zucchini bread.

Drew recognized Mr. Springer's car in the driveway when they pulled up to Lily's house. He'd heard the story of how Lily and Mr. Springer had met – it was part of Lily's explanation of Jeremy's autism and why she was so sensitive to how people reacted to him -- but Drew hadn't quite figured out until that moment that Mr. Springer was dating Lily's mom. It hadn't occurred to him that Mr. Springer would be there for dinner as well and it was a little weird seeing him in that way, and thinking of him as having a life outside of teaching and coaching SCRABBLE. Kind of like realizing, during the FLEBHS class (Charlotte's version of Sex Ed) in 5th grade that your parents had done the deed, at least once or, in the case of Michael Keough, who looked like he was about to throw up, at least *six* times!

Lily opened the door before they'd even had a chance to ring the doorbell and Drew stopped thinking about Mr. Springer.

She was wearing a pretty blouse with little blue flowers on it that magnified the blue of her eyes (she confided later, when Drew mustered up the courage to compliment her on her outfit, that her mom had made her change out of the ratty, but oh so comfortable, t-shirt she'd had on) and her blonde hair was pulled back in a ponytail but little wisps had escaped to frame her forehead.

"Hey Drew," she said, extending her left elbow and sticking out her pinkie for Drew to entwine in his own.

Mara and Sam Founts-Hiltone looked on, a bewildered smile on their faces.

"It's our special handshake we came up with at the Raleigh tournament," Drew explained sheepishly, more than a little embarrassed but also pleased that Lily remembered.

"It's reserved for all those who have taken down Nasty Neil," Lily added, extending her hand to Drew's parents. "I'm sure you heard all about Nasty Neil, right?"

"Oh yes," Mara said, sticking out her left elbow. "I think those of us who gave birth to the Nasty Neil victors should get to do the special handshake too."

Drew just rolled his eyes but Lily went along with it, laughing.

"And how about those who played SCRABBLE with him until he got all competitive about it and now kicks our butts shamelessly? Does that count too?" Sam Founts-Hiltone asked, also sticking out his left elbow.

"Sure, sure," Lily said, playing along, "Sounds fair to me."

"This club is getting bigger by the minute," Drew commented. He kind of liked it just being a special thing between him and Lily.

"And this is my mom," Lily said, as Sally Mallovari walked over from the kitchen.

"Come one in," Sally said, gesturing for them to come inside. "It's so nice to meet you. And good to see you again, Drew."

Everyone entered the Mallovari home and Sally graciously accepted the Founts-Hiltone offerings. "If I'd known I'd get all these goodies," Sally said, "I'd entertain more often."

"If this is as tasty as that pumpkin bread you sent with us to Raleigh," Lily gushed, plucking the zucchini bread from her mother's arms, "then I claim this all to myself. That was sooo good."

Mara smiled and told Lily she'd be happy to share the recipe. She made sure not to look in Drew's direction so that she couldn't be accused of any *I told you so* gloating.

"And I guess you already know Elliott," Sally said, as he, too, emerged from the kitchen, wiping his hands on an apron.

Drew's parents adored Elliott Springer. Had he only taught Drew Latin, he would have been revered (*adj,* regarded with great respect) enough, because he was one of the few middle school teachers who had truly challenged their son intellectually and adjusted the curriculum to continue to do just that as Drew progressed at a much faster clip than anticipated. But the fact that he had also corralled Drew into joining the SCRABBLE Club, and introduced him to the world of competitive SCRABBLE, not to mention forging the first real friendship Drew had managed to start developing outside of Randolph (something Dr. Anderson had strongly encouraged them to pursue for their socially struggling son, but something they had failed at engineering, such as the disastrous Jammin' at the J evening, when he'd refused to talk to them for the entire rest of the weekend), well, Elliot Springer had achieved a gold star in the Founts-Hiltone household.

"Oh yes," Mara gushed, engulfing Elliott in a big bear hug. "The teacher of the year, as far as I'm concerned."

Sally's eyes twinkled as she looked on. She was pretty convinced Elliott was a keeper, but it was nice to see outside validation of what a great guy he was.

After dinner (it turned out ribmaster was another title the Teacher of the Year deserved), the adults adjourned to the living room for coffee while Drew and Lily took on Jeremy in a game of SCRABBLE. Drew wanted to first finish his bowl of blackberry cobbler, but Lily explained to him that there was a timetable that had to be followed.

"Remember how I told you how much he likes routine?" she whispered to Drew, pointing with her eyes at Jeremy, who was proceeding to set up the board on the table that had been cleared in the nick of time. "Well, SCRABBLE is at 7:45. Not *around* 7:45. *At* 7:45."

"That is just so fascinating," Mara marveled, as Sally excused herself to get the hot chocolate ready. "The human mind is such a wondrously complex thing, isn't it?"

"That it is," Elliott Springer agreed. He had come to admire the mystery and complexity of not only Jeremy's brain and his coping mechanisms, but those of his adoring and patient mother and sister as well. The whole family was pretty incredible.

At dinner, when Lily and Drew had compared notes on their respective middle schools, each maintaining that theirs had the highest ratio of idiots in the 8th grade, Elliott heard for the first time some of the indignities Drew had suffered as a result of what he himself called his "supreme nerdiness."

"You should ask them if they like Ben & Jerry's ice cream," Lily suggested.

Drew was not the only one who looked at her as if her elevator wasn't reaching the top floor.

"Remember that movie we saw at the Ben & Jerry's plant in Vermont last year?" Lily said, giggling at all the quizzical looks directed at her. "Well, both Ben & Jerry were major nerds in high school. Like way more than you, Drew."

Drew wasn't sure whether to be flattered or not by the comparison. And he still wasn't sure how that was supposed to help him with the Randolph bullies.

"But now who's got the last laugh?" Elliott said, seeing where Lily was going with it. "They stayed true to themselves and they're now hugely successful."

"Yeah, yeah, the nerds are going to rule the world," Drew said, having discussed this inevitability with Aidan on many occasions, "but that's only if we're able to survive middle school."

All of the adults sighed.

Sally smiled kindly at Mara. She knew what it was like to want to shield your child from pain.

"The good news," she told Mara, when they were chatting after dinner, while Elliott and Sam did the dishes and the kids were playing SCRABBLE, "is that Drew will get through this in a year or two."

Mara nodded sympathetically. She knew what Sally meant, and it came across as far more reassuring and genuine than the platitudes (*n,* a pointless, unoriginal or empty comment or statement made as though it was significant or helpful) usually offered when well-meaning folks assured her that Drew's social awkwardness wouldn't last. Here was someone whose parenting challenge would never end. There would be no temporary awkward phase for Jeremy. No turnaround or societal payback for his current struggles. Seeing him, and Sally's stoic acceptance of his limitations, made Mara's heart ache.

"Lily is such a delight," Mara said, looking admiringly at Sally's bright and vivacious daughter. "And," she added, whispering conspiratorially, "I'm pretty sure I'm not the only member of my family who thinks so."

They both looked over at Drew and Lily and smiled. Mara's son and Sally's daughter were bent over their shared rack of tiles, their heads touching and their brows furrowed (*adj,* wrinkled) identically. Lily said something they couldn't hear and they watched as Drew nodded emphatically (*adv,* with great force or definiteness), grinned from ear to ear, and then clapped her on the back.

Truth was, Drew was having a hard time concentrating on good plays during the SCRABBLE game. As if sitting next to Lily and playing *with* her, their knees touching and her whispered suggestions for possible plays in his ear, wasn't distracting enough, he was completely mesmerized (*adj,* enthralled) with Jeremy's incredible SCRABBLE prowess. Watching him whip his tiles around on his rack and plunk down one bingo after another, not to mention a total of seven words Drew had never heard of and would never have known were actual words but for Lily's assurance that challenging them was not in their best interest, was something Drew could have done for hours. In a way, he envied Jeremy's insular world, his ability to fully concentrate on the task at hand without any regard for how he was perceived and what his social status was in the world around him.

After the game, which Jeremy won handily despite some good plays from the Drew and Lily team, Jeremy asked Drew if he liked to anagram.

"Yeah, but I'm not very good at it," Drew admitted. "I hear *you* are."

"Yes, I like anagramming," Jeremy agreed. "And I'm a good annagrammer. I do them every day."

"I do street signs and stuff I see on my bus ride to school," Drew said. "Like Sharon Amity Road is *My Train Has a Door.*"

Lily giggled. "I guess they don't have to really make sense, huh?"

"Not at my level of aptitude," Drew agreed. "It's all I can just to come up with one."

"Jeremy does names. Like newscasters on TV or someone Mom or I mention at dinner. In like a nanosecond. In his head." Drew looked over at Jeremy with awe. "If he asks for someone's last name," Lily continued, "I know he's about to anagram them."

"Full name," Jeremy barked, as if on cue. "What's your full name?"

Drew realized Jeremy was talking to him.

"Drew Red Founts-Hiltone," he stammered. It had never occurred to him to anagram his own name.

Jeremy picked a series of letters from the tile bag much faster than his clumsy hands would seem to allow. He scrunched up his face for a moment, in deep concentration, and then quickly placed them in a row on the board.

Both Drew and Lily walked over to Jeremy's side of the table to read what he'd come up with.

"That's great, Jeremy," Lily said, laughing. Spontaneously taking Drew's hand in her own, she lofted it high and cried out, "Hear! Hear!"

Never was it cooler to be a nerd. Drew made up his mind then and there to spend as much time as possible with Lily. *And* Jeremy.

On the board, Jeremy had spelled out NERDS OF THE WORLD UNITE.

CHAPTER ELEVEN

"Just make sure you leave your cups of punch on the table," Mr. Springer cautioned everyone. "We don't need any big, red sticky splotches on our thank you letters."

Drew waited his turn to shuffle around the table on which the many thank you letters were placed, each awaiting a signature from him and the other SCRABBLE Club members.

"Someone took the pen for the Walmart letter," Jennifer piped up. "Should I just use the one next to the one for the PTA?"

"No, here you go," Mr. Springer said, collecting the pen from across the table. "Let's try to keep each pen by its corresponding letter so that they look nice and neat." He smiled as he surveyed all the signatures in progress. "And here's my official thank you to all of you," he added, "for your fabulous fundraising efforts. You just didn't take no for an answer and now we have…"

"One thousand nine hundred and forty-seven dollars!" the club members yelled out in unison. They had already totaled the contributions at the start of their send-off party, and they delighted in saying the amount out loud.

Walmart was at the top of the list with a whopping $800 donation. Most of the bookstores gave them small donations, no more than $100, but, as Mr. Springer repeatedly told them, "every little bit counts." Joseph Beth Booksellers explained to Cecelia that they couldn't write her a check but they could donate up to $100 in books. Undeterred, Cecelia selected several beautifully illustrated travel books and brought them in to SCRABBLE Club, suggesting they auction them off to the highest bidder. Mark accused her of playing without all the tiles on her rack ("SCRABBLE humor," Aidan commented, "gotta love it.") but she ended up bringing in the second largest donation thanks to an anonymous bidder (who turned out to be not so anonymous, since Lucy saw the books in Mrs. Villory's office later that week) who wrote out a check for an astonishing $500.

Aidan and Drew struck out at Harris Teeter and Target (something about far away corporate offices and missed deadlines for grant applications) but they set up a lemonade stand that also featured Aidan's mom's heeathbar brownies and a big sign that spelled out L E M O N A D E using oversized SCRABBLE tiles and made three hundred and seventeen dollars and twenty-one cents (the last coming from Jenna Culver, who said that was all she had because her parents had made her allowance contingent (*adj,* dependent on or resulting from a future and as yet unknown event or circumstance) on getting along with her younger brother so she never got it anymore.

"I can't believe you guys made that much," David commented, offering Drew his hand for a high-five. "I'm gonna do some lemonade stands the next time I need money for something, that's for sure."

"Yeah, but you'll need Aidan's mom's heathbar brownies," Drew piped up, wondering again where the heck Aidan was. It was not like him to miss SCRABBLE Club, especially so close to the tournament and especially when Mr. Springer had pretty much promised them a party to celebrate all the money they'd brought in.

"Hey Mr. Springer," Marcus said, holding up one of the letters he had just signed, "it says here that we will be acknowledging their support at the tournament. What's that mean?"

"It means," Mr. Springer said, pulling a cardboard box out from behind the Media Center counter, "that you will each be sporting one of these." He held up a bright blue t-shirt. On the front it said, in SCRABBLE tiles, RMS SCRABBLE CLUB and, underneath that, also in tile letters, WE ALWAYS HAVE THE LAST WORD On the back was written, "Thank you to our sponsors," and each one of the contributors was listed, including "Drew and Aidan's Lemonade Stand." It made it look so official. "We're, like, a company," Drew mused, wondering again why Aidan wasn't there to enjoy the moment with him.

Everyone oohed and ahhed and immediately put their t-shirts on over what they were wearing. Brandon told Lucy that she looked really nice in hers and then she looked even nicer when she smiled and blushed in response. Mohammed grabbed the wrong size at first and proclaimed, "This don't fit!" as he tried squeezing into it, but he then traded with Cecelia, whose extra-large looked like a dress (but not before they both posed for a photo and everyone laughed at how ridiculous they looked). Mr. Springer pulled out another box and handed out the same t-shirts in green, so that they'd have one to wear on the second day of the tournament as well. "I've seen the way you guys eat," he said, "and I knew there was no way one shirt would survive three meals unscathed."

Mrs. Villroy showed up after the t-shirts were distributed with a large sheet cake that was decorated like a big SCRABBLE board. "This is to wish you all luck," she said. "I am just so proud that we have so many teams representing us at such a prestigious (*adj*, having a distinguished reputation) competition and I can't wait to hear all about it when you get back."

"Plus we'll be coming back with the trophy," Marcus predicted. "Drew and Aidan are gonna win the whole thing."

"No we're not," Drew said for the nine millionth time. He had been out there in the SCRABBLE world. He knew that he was the best SCRABBLE player at Randolph, with Aidan a close second, but he didn't know how to let his fellow club members know, without totally offending them or hurting their feelings, that that was not saying much.

"Hey, where *is* Aidan?" Lucy asked.

Everyone looked around, then looked at Drew expectantly.

Drew shrugged his shoulders in the universal "I don't know" gesture and looked at Mr. Springer, who also shook his head.

"I'll take his t-shirts," Drew said, "and give them to him at school tomorrow."

"And give him grief for missing the party," David suggested.

"I'll take his cake," Mohammed piped up, and managed to finagle (*v*, to trick, cheat, or manipulate somebody in order to obtain or achieve something) a second piece from Mrs. Villroy. "With lots of frosting this time, please," he added.

CHAPTER TWELVE

"Is this your bag?" the TSA screener asked, looking at Drew suspiciously.

"Um, yeah," Drew replied, trying not to sound as nervous as he felt.

The metal detector alone had made his heart race. It didn't take much to unleash the foreboding (*n,* a feeling that something bad is going to happen) that seemed to lurk just beneath his skin, ready to spring forth at the slightest hint of trouble. He'd been consumed with a fear that he'd been caught at something, as if he had something to hide, as soon as his backpack had failed to emerge from the x-ray machine. It had been stuck in there, the subject of intense scrutiny, for what seemed like an eternity (*n,* infinite time).

"Step aside, please," the screener said, his tone stern and serious.

Drew felt that familiar pit begin to form in his stomach. The one that signaled impending doom to the rest of his body, which then responded with sweat and a heart rate that Drew was sure could be seen through his shirt.

"Did I do something wrong?" he asked, looking around to see if anyone else was getting pulled out of line. They were not. He had thrown out his water bottle while still in line, following the lead of the people in front of him, and he even doubled checked that he didn't have any of the items listed on the warning signs along the way. Mr. Springer assured the team they didn't have to worry about what was packed in their suitcases since those were getting checked.

"I need some backup here," the screener said to his right shoulder. He appeared to have a small radio transmitter clipped there, so he was able to summon reinforcements – as if he wasn't doing a fine job all by himself of intimidating Drew – without using his hands.

"What's going on?" Mr. Springer asked, having finally noticed that his star SCRABBLE player was about to get arrested or pass out from fear of getting arrested or both.

"Are you with him?" the TSA officer asked, motioning to Drew.

"Yes, I am," Mr. Springer replied. "What seems to be the problem?"

"We have an unidentified object in his bag here," the officer replied, his mustache quivering with the severity of the situation.

Drew looked at Mr. Springer helplessly and raised his shoulders in the universal "I don't know *what* he's talking about" symbol. He racked his brain for everything he'd stuffed in his backpack. There was a copy of Ray Bradbury's *Farenheit 451*, his iPod, *the Official SCRABBLE Players' Dictionary, Fourth Edition*, a sweatshirt his mom had insisted he travel with in case he got cold, and a bag of his mom's homemade trail mix (honey sesame sticks, m&m's, popcorn, yogurt covered raisins, potato sticks and cashews). He'd shared some with Lily and Mr. Springer on their way up to Raleigh and they'd both raved about it so much that he'd asked his mom to make him some for the Rhode Island trip. "Food's okay," Mr. Springer assured him. "It's just liquids they don't want you to bring." But now Drew was convinced he was wrong. Food was *not* okay, and he was in big trouble.

"What *are* those things," the newly-arrived TSA officer asked of the mustached-officer who had summoned him.

A third officer, who had come running, as if Drew's bag might contain a bomb that could detonate at any moment, shook his head in bewilderment. "I've never seen that before."

Drew looked behind him at the line that was swelling with impatience and in front of him, where the rest of his team, who had somehow managed to sail through security just fine, sat laughing at him and conjecturing what kind of sneaky terrorist he was, and he wanted to shrivel up and disappear. Why, oh why, did these kinds of things always seem to happen to him?

He looked up at Mr. Springer for help, a reassuring wink or even a hug, but his teacher's body was twisted across the conveyer belt so that he could sneak a peek at the screen that everyone was staring at with such consternation (*n,* a feeling of bewilderment and dismay, often caused by something unexpected). And then Mr. Springer began to laugh. He was *laughing.*

"Hey Drew," Mr. Springer asked, still laughing. "Did you by any chance happen to bring those racks you won at the Raleigh tournament?"

Drew started to say no, but then he remembered that he'd stuffed them in the front pocket of his backpack in Raleigh and had never removed them. They were long and oversized to allow for greater facility (*n,* an ability to do something easily) in moving one's tiles around to form bingos, and they were made of a heavy wood (rather than the cheap plastic ones he used at school) and painted black. Drew had totally forgotten about the racks, his prize for having the highest scoring word in his division at the Raleigh tournament.

"Those are SCRABBLE tile racks," Mr. Springer, who was still chuckling, told the three TSA officers.

They all stared at him blankly.

"They're *what?*" the mustached-officer asked. He was still looking at Drew as if he was a huge security threat.

"Racks for tiles. For the game of SCRABBLE." Mr. Springer explained. "That's what we're all headed to go and do," he added, motioning to the rest of the team, who were gathered against the wall, watching the proceedings with great amusement. "I'm the coach of our school's SCRABBLE Club and we're off to go play in the National School SCRABBLE tournament in Rhode Island."

"SCRABBLE, huh?" one of the officers asked. "I never knew there were, like, competitions."

"My mom loves that game," the now-smiling mustached-officer said. "She's always trying to get me to play."

"SCRABBLE tile racks," the third officer said, holding up the racks for all to see. "That's a new one."

When they'd returned the racks to Drew's backback and returned the backpack to Drew and Drew was able to breathe normally again and rejoin the rest of the RMS SCRABBLE Club, who cheered and applauded as he walked over to them, embarrassing him further but also making him feel like he belonged, like he was part of a team, he was finally able to laugh about the whole incident.

"It's pretty ironic," he told Lily, when they were seated on the plane, enjoying the Mara Founts-Hiltone Trail Mix along with their complimentary glasses of Sprite, "that quagmire is the word that did me in."

"What do you mean?" Lily asked.

"That's the word I played in Raleigh for 130 points," Drew explained. "It was on a double double."

"Yeah, so?" Lily asked, picking out the M& Ms from the bag.

"That's what won me the high word prize. That's how I got those racks that were such a huge security risk."

Lily smiled at the memory. Drew had been so scared and flustered.

"And do you know what it means?" he asked, when Lily didn't seem to appreciate the full extent of the irony.

"Not really," she admitted. "But I know how to find out." Lily pulled the Official SCRABBLE Players Dictionary out of Drew's backpack and began leafing through the pages.

"Quagmire," she read aloud. "Noun. An area of marshy ground."

She looked at Drew quizzically.

"That's not the only definition," Drew said, laughing.

He asked Mr. Springer, who was sitting across the aisle in 12 E, if he could quickly look up the word quagmire on his laptop's dictionary. "And just read us the second definition," Drew instructed him.

"Quagmire," Mr. Springer said, "An awkward, complicated, or dangerous situation from which it is difficult to escape."

Lily giggled with appreciation. "That's perfect, Drew," she said.

Perfect. That was also a good way to describe the fact that Lily was sitting next to him, in seat 12B, en route to Providence. When Aidan hadn't shown up at school the day after the SCRABBLE party and hadn't returned Drew's calls, Drew had feared the worst. "I'm sure everything's fine," Mara assured him, but Drew knew something was wrong. And it gave him no pleasure to be proven right.

"It's a bad break," Aidan's mom explained, when she finally reached them that evening. She was referring to Aidan's leg, which was broken in two places and was in a heavy-duty cast that went up to his thigh, but also to the fact that he would not be able to go to Rhode Island. "I'm really sorry, Drew. I know you were counting on Aidan to be your partner." She sighed. "Aidan is pretty devastated too, but the doctor said there is no way he can travel any time soon."

Devastated did not even begin to describe how Drew felt. It wasn't just that Aidan was one of his few friends at Randolph and that their partnership extended beyond the SCRABBLE Club. And it wasn't that Aidan was a strong SCRABBLE player, with whom Drew stood the best chance of faring well at the tournament. It was that the other teams were already formed and registered, and everyone from the SCRABBLE Club who wanted to go to the tournament or was able to go had already partnered up. Drew was without a partner. No partner meant no tournament, because you weren't allowed to play by yourself. Mr. Springer checked as soon as he heard the news and it was a no go. The rules were the rules.

Drew hadn't realized how much he'd been looking forward to the tournament until it was yanked from him.

"Maybe you can go as some sort of assistant coach," Sam Founts-Hiltone suggested.

"It's *such* bad luck," Mara agreed, looking sympathetically at her inconsolable (*adj,* so deeply distressed that nobody can offer any effective comfort) son. "But surely Mr. Springer will find a way to let you play."

"No, he *won't,* Mom," Drew spat out. He knew it wasn't her fault, but he had to vent his frustration and anger and well-meaning moms made for easy targets. "There's nothing he can do."

But Drew was wrong. And he was never happier to be wrong.

Mr. Springer summoned him out of third block the next day, showing up in the middle of Science class to ask Mrs. Hughes if he could steal Drew Founts-Hiltone for a moment. Out in the hallway, he shared his good news, his whole face smiling with pride at the solution he'd engineered.

"I checked with the School SCRABBLE folks," he explained, "and it turns out you can have students from two different schools playing together as a team. As long as they only represent one school at the tournament, they don't technically both have to be students at that one school."

Drew was trying to follow what Mr. Springer was telling him. He wasn't particularly thrilled to be paired with someone from another school, someone he didn't even know, but *a p*artner – no matter how undesirable – was better than *no* partner.

"And I asked Lily and she said yes!" Mr. Springer announced, beaming. "She's fine with representing Randolph."

Lily? Lily! *Lily* was his new partner!

"So I guess," Drew told Dr. Anderson, trying to describe his euphoria (*n,* a feeling of great joy, excitement, or well-being), "that things actually do work out sometimes."

Dr. Anderson winked at Drew, as if they were both in on a private joke that no one else understood.

"Yes, they do," he agreed. "Yes, they do."

CHAPTER THIRTEEN

"Sweet. Look at that," Marcus said, pointing to the top of the Rhode Island Convention Center, where a flashing neon screen read WELCOME NATIONAL SCHOOL SCRABBLE CHAMPIONSHIP. Everyone whooped and hollered and high fived each other, except for David, who was solemnly (*adv*, demonstrating sincerity and gravity) taking it all in.

David's eyes grew big as they rode on three massive escalators to reach the top floor of the convention center, where the two-day tournament would be held. He'd thought they'd be playing at the Providence Biltmore Hotel, which was impressive enough, with its ornate (*adj*, with elaborate or excessive decoration), spacious rooms and a doorman who'd greeted David as *Sir*, so when they'd headed out that morning after breakfast to scope out the site of the tournament, he'd expressed surprise.

At breakfast, when Mr. Springer had asked him what he was thinking about, David replied, "That was the most comfortable bed I've ever slept in. I wish I could take it home with me."

"I'm glad *you* slept well," Mohammed quipped. "Because I didn't sleep a wink. *Somebody*," he paused to look pointedly at David, "snores like a banshee."

David wondered if he was, in fact, still dreaming when they registered and were each handed a duffle bag full of goodies. Not one per team, but one per *player*, filled with more presents than David received at Christmas! There was a School SCRABBLE t-shirt, a word game called Boggle, some SCRABBLE pencils and a notepad, a folder full of information about the tournament, a copy of *The Official SCRABBLE Players Dictionary, 4th Edition*, and something that looked like some kind of Gameboy. David was a little disappointed when Drew explained that it was an electronic dictionary.

"Another dictionary?" he asked, thinking one was more than enough. "They already gave us one."

"Yeah, but this one is electronic," Drew replied, scrambling to find his in his own duffle bag. "It's called a Franklin, and it's basically like having your own Zyzzyva."

"Like let's say you're wondering if, oh, I don't know, *overstay* is good," Lily piped up. She had quickly established herself as a strong SCRABBLE player who knew all sorts of neat words and tricks, and the rest of the Randolph SCRABBLE Club, who'd been dubious at first about letting someone from Crestdale join their team, had made room for her next to Drew on the SCRABBLE pedestal. "You can type it in and it'll tell you instantly if it's acceptable or not."

"And you can anagram with it," a small man who looked like a younger version of Mr. Burns from *The Simpsons* said. He had walked up to join their group while Drew and Lily were touting the merits of the Franklin. "I find it most useful as a quick way of seeing if I've missed any words that were on my rack. You just type in the letters you have and it'll spit back to you all the words you could have made."

"Cool," Jennifer said, trying to break open the plastic on her Franklin. "This'll help me a ton during the tournament. I still haven't memorized my threes."

"Oh, you can't use it during the tournament," the young Mr. Burns said, shaking his head in disgust. "That'd be cheating."

He walked off without another word.

"They'll go over all that with you," Mr. Springer told them. "Anything at all that could be used to look up a word, even a cell phone, has to be turned off."

"Who *was* that?" Lucy asked.

"Probably another coach," Mohammed mused.

"No," Mr. Springer said, whispering theatrically. "That was Joe Shoeman."

His students just stared at him.

"*Joe Shoeman,*" he said again. "As in *the* Joe Shoeman. He's a National as well as a World SCRABBLE Champion."

"He looks kinda old." David commented. "He must have won it a long time ago."

"No, not the School SCRABBLE Championship," Mr. Springer corrected him. "He won playing against *adults.* He now works for the

National SCRABBLE Association. He has made a career out of playing SCRABBLE."

"Whoa," Marcus said with awe. He was wondering if professional SCRABBLE could serve as his backup to his professional basketball aspirations (*n, pl,* earnest desires or ambitions).

"He may be good at SCRABBLE," Jennifer muttered, "But he's a little weird."

"Over here, kids," a cheery woman sporting an enormous camera called out to them. "Team photo time."

They all had their photos taken, each pair striking its own unique pose.

David and Mohammed, despite their reverence (*n,* feelings of deep respect or devotion) for the hotel, the tournament and the fact that they were actually there, were able to tap into their inner goofiness and make silly faces. Mohammed cocked his head, bugged out his eyes and stuck his tongue out while David puckered his lips as if he was about to kiss Mohammed.

Mr. Springer shook his head, pretending to be dismayed with their behavior, but he was actually glad they were starting to relax and enjoy themselves.

Brandon and Lucy looked less awkward than they usually did together. Lucy smiled shyly, staring straight at the camera, seemingly oblivious (*adj,* forgetting everything or being unaware of surroundings) to her partner's crush on her, while Brandon looked adoringly at her. "Face forward," the nice photographer lady admonished (*v,* to rebuke somebody mildly but earnestly) him. "I know she's cute and all, but we need a shot of your face, not your profile."

"Ooh, busted," David teased, while Mohammed barked like a dog.

The result was matching blushes for their snapshot. True partners.

Marcus and Irwin were all business. They had won their last game at SCRABBLE Club and were pumped and ready to go. They would not necessarily have picked each other as partners, but they had grown to appreciate each other as players and they were each secretly relieved they had not been paired with a girl.

Feeling similarly fortunate that their partnership did not cross gender lines were Cecelia and Jennifer. Cecelia looked back at the camera, her mind full of the short X words and Q without a U words she'd just studied that morning before breakfast. Jennifer, meanwhile, was wondering if Mr. Springer would let them hit the mall that was attached to the Convention Center during their lunch break.

The last pair to be photographed was Lily and Drew. Lily sported her RMS SCRABBLE shirt proudly, and Drew marveled at her ability to fit in with such ease while he, who had attended Randolph since the 6th grade, still struggled mightily. She had simply added a piece of masking tape, on which she'd written, in small letters, "NOT" under the Randolph logo. The ease with which she'd reconciled not attending the school she was representing, and the way she'd still managed to express herself, and retain her identity while simultaneously fitting in with a group of kids she'd only just met, impressed the heck out of Drew.

Little did he know that it was more of a struggle than she let on. She'd actually said no when Elliott first broached her with the idea. It's not that she had any fierce loyalty to Crestdale or a deep desire to represent her school, but it seemed disingenuous (*adj,* giving a false impression of sincerity or simplicity) to represent Randolph, a school she had never attended at all. And as much as she had come to love Elliott and consider him a member of her family, she wasn't sure she was keen on spending a weekend with him away from home where she'd have to share him with a bunch of kids she didn't know and navigate the awkward line between the way she knew him and related to him and the way the students whom he taught and coached did. What Drew didn't realize most of all, and if he had, he would have looked at Lily with even more awe and wonderment than he already did, was that what had clinched it for her, what had made her overcome her misgivings and say yes, I'll do it, was *him.* When Elliott told her that Drew would be unable to compete without a partner, and knowing, as she did, that not just any partner would do, but one who could actually contribute, so that it wasn't just Drew out there, playing solo with a warm body next to him who was simply trying not to get in the way, well, she just had to say yes. Drew deserves this, she thought, and it secretly thrilled her that she was in a position to give it to him. Her loyalty to her friend, which surprised her in its intensity given that they had only known each other a few months, ran deeper than any of her misgivings. And once she'd committed, and heard his breathless gratitude and excitement when he'd called her after hearing the news, there was no turning back. As she explained to Samantha and Jessie, it was as if she and Drew, and the entire RMS SCRABBLE Club, once she'd met them and been so readily accepted into their ranks, were a third and separate entity to which they all belonged.

Looking at his partner, her mouth open in laughter at David's antics (*n,* acts in a clownish manner), her blue eyes open with excitement, Drew felt his heart begin to race. It was akin to what he'd felt in the security line at the Charlotte Douglas Airport, only slightly more pleasant. A long time ago, when he'd confessed to his mom that he did not really feel romantically towards anyone, thinking at the time that it was yet one more thing that was wrong with him, that set him apart from the other, normal middle schoolers at Randolph, Mara had reassured him that he was simply a late bloomer. "When someone special, boy or girl, makes your heart go pit a pat," she said, "you'll know." Drew thought it was an inane Momism way back then, but now he got it.

And as he smiled into the camera, he felt thankful that there was no bubble above his head letting everyone know what he was thinking. Because what he thought, as he felt his pulse quicken in what was now a familiar sensation whenever he was near Lily, was, "You make my heart go pit a pat."

CHAPTER FOURTEEN

"We have one hundred and four teams here this year," John Williams, the Executive Director of the National SCRABBLE Association, told the hushed ballroom full of players, parents and coaches. The players were all seated at their assigned tables, having already introduced themselves to their opponents, and the coaches and parents lined the perimeter of the room, relegated to the sidelines by a rope barrier they were not allowed to cross. "This year we have participants from 22 states and the District of Columbia," Mr. Williams continued, "and a total of 208 students. This is also the first year every single team who registered showed up, and we are delighted to see all of you here."

Lily looked around the room. She was taking a mental photograph for Jeremy. She wanted him to vicariously (*adv*, experienced through another person rather than at first hand, by using sympathy or the power of the imagination) enjoy the tournament experience with her and she didn't want to forget anything for him, although there were certain things she would intentionally leave out. For instance, there was no need to mention the fact that there was a cap on the cumulative points a team could score, with a 100 point spread the limit for the first game, a 150 point spread for the second game and a 250 point limit for the rest of the games. Lily appreciated why the NSA had imposed the limits, so that an experienced team would not overwhelmingly crush a less experienced team, at least as far as the point spread was concerned, but the reasoning behind the rule change would be completely lost on Jeremy. And the rule change itself – no matter what the reason – would drive him crazy. He was a rule monger, and changing the rules or the system for doing something, once it had been established, sent him into a frenzy (*n*, a state of uncontrolled activity, agitation, or emotion such as excitement or rage).

"Let me see a show of hands," Mr. Williams instructed, "for all of you who have played here before."

Lily and Drew's opponents raised their hands, as did about half of the room.

"Oh good," Lily thought, "I'm not the only newbie here."

"Crap," Drew thought, "we're playing veterans in our very first game. We're going to get our butts kicked."

"And now raise your hands if this is your first time at the National School SCRABBLE Tournament," Mr. Williams said, again surveying the room.

Everyone from the Randolph Middle School SCRABBLE Club raised a hand. Lily was gratified to see how many of the kids at adjoining tables raised their hands. Drew was convinced he saw their opponents look at each other and snicker.

After thanking all of the volunteers, coaches and parents for their efforts in making the sixth annual National School SCRABBLE Championship a success, Mr. Williams informed them he had just one more thing to say. "I say it every year," he said, "but it's important so listen up."

The kids who were eager to get started and had begun to fidget settled down for the big announcement. A hush fell over the room, including among the bystanders who were trying to find good seats. Parents who had staked out chairs that seemed optimal, near the podium and directly behind the rope, were now gathering their things and moving, having discovered too late that their children were playing their first game in an entirely different part of the room and it would be impossible to read their body language and follow what was going on from where they were currently sitting. Mr. Springer, one of the few coaches who had brought five teams (most only brought one or two) had teams spread throughout the room so he opted to sit in the back row with his laptop. He'd know soon enough how everyone had done; no need to frustrate himself with trying to interpret what was going on from afar.

Mr. Williams gripped the sides of the podium with both hands and leaned forward.

"SCRABBLE is fun," he said.

There were a few giggles and a murmuring of comments at some of the tables.

"Of course, you already know that," Mr. Williams conceded. "But I thought I'd remind you because winning is fun too, but very few of you in this room will win a prize here. Some of you may not even win any games."

Drew fervently (*adv,* passionately) hoped that would not be the case for him and Lily.

"But you can lose and still have a great time playing SCRABBLE. You might make a great bingo or a great play. Or you might see a spot for a word you didn't think you'd be able to play."

In his backrow seat, Elliott Springer nodded approvingly. He hoped his players, especially Marcus and Mohammed, who stood a good chance of losing every single game, were listening and absorbing what John Williams was saying. He knew there would be disparities (*n, pl,* lack of equality between things or people) in how the teams from Randolph fared at the tournament, but he wanted it to be a positive experience for all of them. He did, however, harbor (*v,* entertain) high hopes for Lily and Drew. He was perhaps a tad bit biased when it came to both of them, but he was hard-pressed to think of two 8th graders who were smarter or more savvy about the game. Or more deserving of a big win.

Ben Greenwood then took the stage and introduced himself as the tournament's director. He went over some of the rules that were set forth in their packets and reviewed with them how to fill out the paperwork that was on each table, like the challenge slips, the result slips and their score sheets. He went over how to designate blanks ("Say what the blank is before you hit your clock."); the mechanics of a challenge ("One player from each team goes to one of the computers that are set up around the room."); and what to do if there was an issue that could not be resolved by the players ("If at all in doubt, raise your hand and an official – anyone wearing one of these nifty black and white striped referee shirts – will come to your table.").

"The result slips have to be signed by all four of you," Mr. Greenwood informed them. "Don't touch the tiles, the clock or the board until the result slips have been signed off by both teams and verified by an official."

Lily could see some dazed, slightly panicky expressions around her. Even Drew, who had every reason to feel confident and ready, having both tournament experience and the best vocabulary and SCRABBLE prowess of anyone she knew other than Jeremy, looked ready to flee. It was both puzzling and endearing (*adj,* charming) to her that Drew got so easily flustered. Most of the boys she knew at Crestdale were full of bravado and cockiness, whereas Drew – who had so much more cause than they did to brag and posture – was full of doubt and insecurity. Go figure.

"Any questions?" Mr. Greenwood asked the players.

One hand shot up. It was a boy near the back of the room.

"Yes," Mr. Greenwood said, pointing at the boy. "Stand up, please, so we can all hear your question."

The boy stood up and practically yelled, "WHAT IF WE NEED TO GO TO THE BATHROOM?"

CHAPTER FIFTEEN

At five minutes past two (Jeremy would have been in the throes of a meltdown, since the schedule called for play to start at 2:00 pm), Mr. Greenwood announced, "Let the games begin!"

Drew and Lily already knew they were going first. The pairings list on the bulletin board outside Ballroom A, where they were playing, listed not only their opponents (Billingsworth Middle School – Montgomery, Texas) but also their table number and which team would be going first (Randolph Middle School, Team A – Charlotte, NC). Since no one had to draw a tile to determine who would go first and all the score sheets had been readied during the interminable (*adj, so long and boring or frustrating as to seem endless*) opening announcements, all fifty-two tile bags were hoisted in the air at once and the sound of 5,200 tiles simultaneously shaking filled the room.

Lily squeezed Drew's hand, and her eyes matched her words. "Isn't this exciting?" she whispered.

Drew nodded and smiled back. "More than you know," he felt like responding.

Aidan was one of Drew's best friends. Shoot, he was one of Drew's *only* friends. And Aidan was a great SCRABBLE player. He would have made a great partner and, together, they would have been a formidable team. Drew had been truly devastated that Aidan couldn't come to the tournament. He also felt bad for Aidan, stuck back in Charlotte, wanting more than anything to be in Providence, sitting where Lily was sitting right then, next to Drew, at Table Number 77, about to play their first game in the National School SCRABBLE Championship. But watching Lily carefully select seven tiles from the bag and place them face down, her face intense with concentration as she counted to make sure she had not overdrawn, and full of the excitement and anticipation for the game, the tournament and the fact that he was sharing both with the smartest and prettiest girl in the room, well, Drew was convinced that Aidan's broken leg was a major bummer for Aidan, but it was pretty much the best thing that had ever happened to Drew.

"Ugh," Lily whispered, as she placed I U G L R E and another U on their rack.

"Maybe we should trade," Drew suggested, shielding his mouth with his hand so that the Billingsworth team couldn't hear him. No need for them to know how bad their opening rack was. He remembered reading in EVERYTHING SCRABBLE, a book he'd received for Chanukah from Uncle Ben, that the best time to trade was your first turn, if you were going first. It was basically akin to starting over again and simply going second instead of first. You had little to lose.

"Wait a minute," Lily said, shuffling the tiles around the way her big brother was wont (*adj,* accustomed or likely to do something) to do. She showed her six-letter word to Drew, and he nodded his assent.

"Good find," he said, as Lily placed U G L I E R on the board. "Sixteen."

"Yes!" the Billingsworth boys both said at once. The one who had introduced himself as Nick didn't even hesitate before putting their letters – all seven – on the board. "We were hoping you'd play a G," he confessed. He placed T H A N K I N above Drew's and Lily's G.

The other boy, whose nametag said MATT CABOT and whose role during the remainder of the game appeared to be little more than scorekeeper, tallied the points. "Let's see," he said, trying unsuccessfully to sound nonchalant (*adj,* calm and unconcerned about things). "Sixteen doubled is thirty-two," he paused, looking back at the word to make sure he'd added it up right, "plus fifty is eighty-two."

One thing Drew had learned in the two tournaments he now had under his belt is that a game can have many reversals of fortune. There was no such thing as an insurmountable (*adj,* impossible to overcome or deal with successfully) lead, especially this early in the game, so he was not ready to despair. Yet.

"It's okay," he whispered to Lily, wanting more than anything to reassure *her,* to make sure *she* wasn't giving up.

Lily wasn't listening, though. She wasn't despairing either. What she was doing was moving their tiles around on their rack.

"How about this?" she said, showing Drew the A and X on their rack and then pointing at the H and A in THANKING. "The A is on the triple letter square going both ways, so that's six plus the X both ways for sixteen plus five for the A and the H, that's, um, twenty-seven points."

"Not bad," Drew agreed, "but over here," he said, motioning to the triple letter square above the I in UGLIER, "is even better."

He placed an N above the U in UGLIER (NU – *n*, the 13th letter of the Greek alphabet, represented in the English alphabet as "n"), an E above the L (EL – *n*, the letter L), and an X above the I (XI – *n*, the 14th letter of the Greek alphabet, represented in the English alphabet as "x"). He then put an A in front of it all to form the word ANNEX (*v*, to attach something subsidiary to a larger thing), using the N that was already above the G from their opponents' 82-point play, for a total of 42 points.

"You rock!" Lily said, her voice full of admiration.

Drew had never felt like the things he was good at, almost all of them academic, carried much social cache. If anything, they only dragged him down socially, reinforcing his status as nerd of all nerds. But with Lily, who patted his leg affectionately as she wrote down their score (now a much more respectable 58 points), he felt so thankful for his SCRABBLE skills.

Both teams made some more good plays, each using the blank to bingo later in the game (FANCIER for the Billingsworth boys and MINERAL for Drew and Lily) and it continued to be anyone's game most of the way through, each team taking the lead only to have the other team steal it back a turn or two later. With only six tiles left in the bag, the score was 353 for Billingsworth and 340 for Randolph. Two power tiles were still out: the J and the Q. The J was on Drew's and Lily's rack, and Drew wanted to play it to form the word JOIN, with the N in MINERAL, for 27 points because the J would be on the triple letter square. Lily disagreed.

"The Q is still out," she pointed out. "We should block that I so that they don't have a place to play it and they get stuck with it."

The spot she was referring to would only yield 10 points for the word JIN. It would not even be enough to catch them up, let alone allow them to take the lead the way Drew's play would.

"Yeah, but the Q might still be in the bag and *we* could still get it," Drew whispered back. "Then we've blocked ourselves *and* lost out on a good play."

Lily cast a nervous glance at the clock. She didn't want to waste too much time deliberating their move.

"Do what you want to do," she said. "I trust you."

And because he believed her, Drew played JIN for 10 points.

The Billingsworth Boys' look of dismay said it all. Lily's gut had been right. They had the Q.

From that point on, each team made small, piddly plays, with the Billingsworth team trying to create an opening for their Q and Drew and Lily blocking any possible Q dumps while chipping away at the lead. The final score, when Drew and Lily went out with VIBE (*n,* a particular kind of atmosphere, feeling, or ambience), was 382 for Billingsworth and 378 for Randolph.

Nick practically threw the Q at them.

"You get 10 points for our dang Q," he said, knowing that any tiles left on his rack would be added to his opponents' score and subtracted from his own.

Lily busied herself with filling out the results slip so that she would not appear to be gloating. She recorded 372 for Billingsworth and 388 for Randolph, Team A.

"Good game," Drew said, extending his hand. He meant it, too. That was a nail biter. Close games like that were grueling but ultimately more rewarding, at least when you came out on top.

"Man, I really thought we were going to win that one," Matt said, his hand in his hair. "How'd you do that?"

"Teamwork," Lily said, putting her arm around Drew.

Drew caught Mr. Springer's eye across the room and gave him a thumbs up.

"You're undefeated," he gushed, embracing them both in a bear hug when they rejoined him out in the hallway.

Lily laughed. "Yeah, let's just quit right now. Then we can tell everyone we never lost a single game."

Drew laughed too, but the last thing he wanted to do was quit. Not even in jest (*n,* something done or said in a playful, joking manner).

CHAPTER SIXTEEN

"We didn't get a single blank all day," a short girl with braids and glasses bemoaned.

"Well, we got nothing but vowels in one game," retorted a boy with a very Southern drawl. His nametag indicated he was from Mobile, Alabama. "And then nothing but consonants in our next two."

"Yeah, we had us some baaaaad luck," his partner, wearing an Auburn Tigers hat, agreed.

"Sure wish there were money prizes for *this,*" a heavyset boy playing Connect Four said. "Now *this*, I'm good at!"

"What *I'm* good at," Mohammed said, making the rest of his team crack up as he maneuvered (*v, moving or acting in a way that requires skill or dexterity)* his way around the room and joined them at a large table in the corner, "is making ice cream sundaes."

"That no one but you would want to eat," Mr. Springer added, shaking his head in mock disgust at Mohammed's creation.

There was not a single topping that Mohammed had declined, and he had shown no restraint (*n, an act or the quality of holding back, limiting, or controlling something)* in quantities either. Several scoops of ice cream were buried under oreo cookies chunks, nuts, sprinkles, marshmallow cream, hot fudge, butterscotch, whipped cream, cherries, M&Ms, gummy worms and chocolate covered raisins, all of which were cascading down the sides of his overflowing dish and many of which had created a trail from the ice cream bar to their table.

"Just take a picture of this," Mohammed said, digging in and smiling for a pretend camera, his dripping spoon frozen mid-air, "and put it on your posters next year. That's all you'll need to get kids to join SCRABBLE Club." He took another huge mouthful, and then another. He didn't seem to be making a dent in the mountain of melting ice cream in front of him. "Trust me, don't even do all that

'Do you like to spell' stuff. Just say 'Do you like ice cream?' You'll have 100 teams next year!"

Everyone laughed. Everyone except Lucy and Brandon, who were off playing Pictionary with a team from California whom they'd faced in Game Three.

"Let's go play Twister," Lily suggested. "Come on, Elliott... I mean, Mr. Springer. Drew and I will take you on."

"Uh no, you do *not* want me on your team," Drew assured her. "I'm awful at stuff like that."

"Yeah, when's the last time you played Twister?" Lily shot back. Then, without waiting for Drew to answer, she added, "And who cares? Winning is not the point. Let's just go have some fun."

It appeared that Lucy and Brandon and Mohammed and David agreed. Neither team had won a game and they were among the thirty two teams who were 0 and 3 for the day, but they sure looked like they were having fun. Marcus and Irwin had won their last game, after losing the first two, and Cecelia and Jennifer had won two of their three games. Only Lily and Drew were undefeated, but at the bottom of the cluster of teams who were also undefeated since two of their three games had been squeakers (*n,* a competition, election, race, or other event that is won by a very slight margin) and their point spread was comparatively low.

Drew went to bed contented (*adj,* peacefully happy and satisfied with the way things are, or with what you have done or achieved). The ice cream social had been surprisingly fun, even the game of Twister, despite Drew proving to be as awful at it as he had claimed to be. But Lily didn't seem to care. No one did. That's what made the evening, and the whole tournament, such a new experience for Drew. No one was mocking him. No one was dissing him. And it wasn't like he was invisible, either. He had a hard time going to sleep, what with the excitement of the day, the ice cream he'd eaten so close to bed time, and all the anticipation for day two of the tournament. He knew he needed a good night's sleep, but it was as if the knowing it made it even harder to get it, and then he found himself kept awake by the stress of being kept awake.

His last sensation, before finally falling asleep, was panic that he'd be so tired that he'd oversleep the alarm. He needn't have worried. He awoke on Saturday morning, day two of the tournament, before 5:00 am. He could hear the rest of the guys slumbering away, each with his own characteristic sleep idiosyncrasy (*n,* a way of behaving, thinking or feeling that is peculiar to an individual or group, especially an odd or unusual one). Mohammed made a slight wheezing sound that was annoying at first but quickly became part of the room's background noise. Brandon didn't make a noise but he moved around a lot, which was probably what had woken Drew up since he had the misfortune of sharing a bed with Brandon. And David, his fourth roommate, was a snorer. What was worse, there was no rhythm or system to his snores. He'd let out a loud snort, followed by a prolonged whistle as he blew the air back out, and then he'd do it again maybe three, four times. Then silence, and you'd be convinced he was done and the snoring was over, only to be startled by another loud series of snorts and whistles a few minutes later.

Drew tried going back to sleep, but it was no use. His mind was racing with all that the day had to offer. He couldn't wait to get back in that ballroom at the Rhode Island Convention Center. After lying in bed, his eyes by then wide open and his mind fully alert and beyond any hope of being lulled back to sleep, he decided to go down to the lobby and study the list of J and X words Mr. Springer had given them. JUKU still haunted him. That's what he'd had on his rack in Game 3, and there was a great place to play it, with the J on the triple letter score, but he had chickened out because he couldn't remember if JUKU (*n,* an additional school in Japan for preparing students for college) was a word.

"I've never heard of it," Lily whispered to him, "but that doesn't mean diddly squat. Just go with your gut."

Lily had more confidence in his gut than he did, it turns out. They didn't play the word because Drew wasn't sure and he didn't want to risk it. They played JO (*n,* a sweetheart) instead, for a mere 16 points. After the game, a quick check of his new Franklin (Mr. Springer had kindly purchased triple A batteries for the whole team) revealed that JUKU was fine. "Aargh!" Drew thought. "Aarrgh!" and "Aarrghh!"

He slipped on a pair of shorts and a t-shirt and tried to leave the room without waking up his roommates. There was little danger of disturbing their slumber. On Friday morning, they had managed to sleep through the alarm *and* his shower *and* Mr. Springer's phone call wondering where they were, and it had taken Drew pulling the covers off and yelling their names to get them to even open their eyes. Still, Drew didn't want to give them any reason to dislike him, so he tiptoed around their clothes that were strewn around the room and he carried his shoes out with him so that he wouldn't make noise putting them on. So far, they had been surprisingly decent to him, even though none of them shared his pond scum status at school. They didn't seem to take pleasure in mocking him, the way pretty much everyone else at Randolph did, and for that Drew was immensely (*adv,* to a huge extent or degree) grateful and intent on keeping it that way.

When he got to the lobby, he was surprised to find it entirely empty. He had only been in and out of the hotel during busy times so he always pictured the lobby full of noise and people, the way it was every time he traipsed (*v,* walked around casually or without a specific destination) through it But when the elevator dinged its arrival and the doors opened, the room was eerily quiet and still. The classical music that Drew barely noticed during the day seemed unusually loud as it echoed across the empty lobby. Drew picked a spot on the plush couch near the huge planter by the registration desk and settled down with his list of words and his Franklin.

It occurred to him that the hotel employees were used to going about their work at that hour unseen and that they were unaware he was sitting there, quietly studying his words. The front desk clerk, a young man with a pathetic excuse for a beard who looked to be not much older than Drew, kept stretching out his mouth in huge, exaggerated yawns, which were punctuated by loud *ooh aahs* and occasionally followed by a head shaking that made his cheeks and lips wobble back and forth, much the way Aidan's dog dried himself off when he emerged from the creek behind Aidan's mom's house.

A woman who was polishing the banisters on the big stairs leading up to the ballroom where the ice cream social had been held kept readjusting the skirt of her Providence Biltmore uniform, which appeared to be too tight. She would pull it down, polish a bit, and then yank on it again, muttering in some Slavic language each time she did.

"Oh meester, I so sorry," the embarrassed cleaning woman said, as she practically ran Drew's feet over with the vacuum cleaner. "I no see you there."

"No problem," Drew said, lifting his feet up.

The front desk clerk looked up, startled, when Drew spoke, suddenly aware that his yawn fest was no longer a private affair.

Drew refocused on his list. He was determined to at least commit the short J words to memory before he went back upstairs to wake up the guys. He then used his Franklin to look up the definitions of any J words he didn't know. There were quite a few. In the JA's alone, there were JAMB (*v,* to jam; to force together tightly); JANE (*n,* a girl or a woman); JAPE (*v,* to mock, ridicule or make fun of); JATO (*n,* a takeoff aided by jet propulsion); JAUK (*v,* to dawdle, to waste time) and JAUP (*v,* to splash, splatter a liquid about).

The elevator dinged and Drew looked up to see a man dressed in running shorts and a t-shirt emerge. He watched as the man did some stretches just outside the sliding glass doors and then took off running down the street. A couple who appeared to have far more luggage than two people should ever need made a noisy entrance a few minutes later and immediately launched into a loud debate with the no-longer yawning front desk clerk about some charges on their bill. Drew was relieved to see a cab pull up and the lobby return to its peaceful, pre-hustle and bustle state after they left.

There were plenty of short X words Drew didn't know yet either. He'd tried to study them on the bus ride to school but the solid command he'd thought he'd had on all the words on the list dissipated (*v,* caused something to fade or disappear) as soon as the tournament started. He began questioning himself, and having a partner – especially one he liked and respected as much as Lily – actually made it worse. He so didn't want to disappoint her or be the reason for their defeat that he would only play a word unless he was absolutely sure of it. And, as it turned out, there were very few words, especially the newest additions to his brain, of which he was very sure. He tried repeating the X words and their definitions out loud, in a low murmur but out loud nonetheless, to help commit them to memory.

"Calx," Drew said, after punching the word in to his Franklin and hitting the dictionary button. "Noun. A mineral deposit." He surveyed the list again, then repeated the process. "Dexy. Noun. A tablet of dex."

"But what the heck is dex?" he wondered out loud.

"It's a sulfate used as a central nervous system stimulant," Lily said, suddenly standing right in front of him.

Drew looked up, startled. She was wearing a tank top, shorts and running shoes, and her face was flushed and sweaty. "What are you doing here?" he managed to ask.

"Well, good morning to you too," Lily said, plopping down next to him. "I was running up and down the stairs. I got up to go for a run but then I decided it was too dark and scary outside, especially considering my penchant for getting lost, so I decided to do the stairs instead."

Drew realized he had it bad. Even drenched in sweat, her hair pulled back in a ponytail and panting from her exertion, Lily looked gorgeous to him.

"I was trying to do some cramming before our big matches today," Drew admitted, sheepishly. "But I think it's a lost cause."

"A lost cause?" Lily asked, punching him on the shoulder. Even though it was meant in jest, and despite the fact that it was a punch rather than something more intimate or tender, the fact that Lily was touching him at all made Drew blush with pleasure. "You'd better leave that pessimism behind in the hotel today, Mister, or I'm getting myself a new partner!"

"Well, I guess we *are* doing pretty well," Drew admitted sheepishly. "Especially considering this is our first time here for both of us."

"You think?" Lily asked, again teasing him. "Elliott told me we've already exceeded his expectations." She took Drew's hand in hers and looked into his eyes. Did she have any clue, any inkling at all, what that did to him? Drew concentrated mightily on not letting his face reflect what he was thinking, because he was pretty sure he would scare her away for good if she had any clue. Suffice it to say his thoughts were not focused on anything having to do with SCRABBLE at the moment. "So let's just enjoy the day and see where it goes," Lily said, her eyes smiling at Drew kindly. "Relax. It's all good."

Lily crossed her legs Indian style and settled in next to Drew on the couch.

"It's kind of fun watching the hotel come to life, isn't it?" she asked.

Drew agreed. He told Lily about the yawning front desk clerk and the cleaning woman with the wedgie problem. "Oh dees underwear ees no fitting me no more," he said, imitating her thick Eastern European accent, spurred on by Lily's laughter.

The runner who had headed out on his run earlier that morning, before Lily had joined Drew in the lobby, returned. He checked his watch, then headed to the elevator.

"Guess I could have run with him," Lily commented, which, for some reason, struck Drew as hysterically funny.

"Uh oh, we've got a case of inexplicable laugher," Lily said, joining in the chuckle fest. "Guess we're both getting it out of our system before the big games today."

"Yeah, we're probably going to have to face the Mitchell twins at some point today," Drew said, feeling the familiar tingle of butterflies in his stomach despite Lily's noble efforts to distract and relax him. "And I guarantee you they are not yukking it up right now."

"Not now or ever," Lily agreed. "I don't think they even know *how* to smile."

"Yeah, they're on a mission," Drew said, repeating what Mr. Springer had told him. "I guess they narrowly lost last year and now they've got something to prove."

"Well, they'll have to get past *us* first," Lily said, putting her arm around Drew.

Drew knew she meant *us* in the most platonic, SCRABBLE-partners kind of way, but it still sounded great to him. He was usually on the outside of any *us*; it felt great to be a part of one, especially when it included someone as fabulous as Lily as part of the equation.

"Okay, we both have to teach each other one cool word trick or thing we know that the other one doesn't before we head up to shower," Lily said, facing Drew, her smile and enthusiasm contagious (*adj,* quickly spread from one person to another). "You never know, it might just be the thing that wins a game for us today."

"Let's see," Drew said, racking his brain for something that would impress Lily. "If *examine* happens to be on the board and we have an H on our rack, we can use the H as a front hook because *hexamine* is also a word."

"Cool," Lily said, nodding with approval. "What's it mean?"

"I don't know," Drew admitted sheepishly. "I just remember that it's a word. Hold on." He took out his Franklin and typed in the word. "Hexamine. Noun. A chemical compound."

"I think that's what every bizarre word means," Lily said, shaking her head.

"Yeah," Drew agreed. "Who knew there were so many chemical compounds out there?"

"Mine comes from Jeremy," Lily said, scrunching up her face with concentration as she tried to remember one of the many things Jeremy had tried to teach her before she'd left for Rhode Island. "Ologies," she said, "which is a bingo with yucky tiles, by the way, means branches of knowledge." Drew nodded, rolling his eyes when Lily added that unlike *some* people, she, at least, knew the meaning of the words she was offering up for his edification (*n,* instruction or enlightenment, especially when it is morally or spiritually uplifting).

"Anyway," she continued, "you can add a second O as a front hook for oologies, studies of birds' eggs, and *then*," her eyes lit up with excitement, "we could add a Z in front of that for zoologies," she paused for dramatic effect. "The sciences of animals."

"Cool," Drew said, and he meant it.

The elevator dinged and a slew of kids emerged, their shirts and bags giving them away as fellow competitors.

"Crap, we'd better get upstairs," Drew said, suddenly realizing how much time had elapsed.

"Time flies when you're studying words," Lily said, following him to the elevator.

"No," Drew thought to himself. "Time flies when you're hanging out with someone you *really, really* like."

CHAPTER SEVENTEEN

At the end of round four, with only two games to go, seven teams were still undefeated. For the first time all weekend, Drew let himself start entertaining the idea that he and Lily could actually win this thing. They had not lost yet, and they seemed to be getting better with every game. They had won their last game, the one before lunch against a team from Darien, Connecticut, with a huge margin. Their score of 689 was not only the highest score of the tournament thus far, but the highest score of any team in the tournament's history. As the rest of the Randolph team high-fived them and other teams and players came by to congratulate them and ask them about the game ("Is it true you bingoed three times?" "Did they really lose four challenges?" "How on earth did you know that oologies is even a word?"), Drew understood that part of his nerves were due to his desire to win. Looking at the ESPN crew circling the tables (even Matt Santoni would have to be impressed – it was ESPN, after all!), Drew suddenly understood how very much he wanted to win. Not just the next game, but the whole tournament. He couldn't remember ever wanting anything more.

He could tell that Lily was caught up in the same excitement.

"I can't eat," she said at lunch. "I'm too nervous."

"What happened to just enjoying the ride," Drew teased her, but he felt the same way. The closer they got to the final four, the more possible winning it all seemed.

When the pairings went up on the board, Lily, who was taller by several inches, was the first to see their fate. Drew could tell by her face, which sported an expression of fear mixed with astonishment, that the pairing was not to her liking.

"We're playing the friggin' Mitchell twins," Lily reported, shaking her head. "Our last game catapulted us into second place. We actually did ourselves a disservice with that one."

Now it was Drew's turn to be cheerleader. He was feeling pumped and uncharacteristically confident.

"We can do this, Lily," he said, taking her hand. When she squeezed his fingers in response, he felt even more raring to go. If there had been a car that needed to be lifted off the ground right at that moment, Drew had no doubt he'd be able to take care of it single-handed. There was no stopping him.

The Mitchell twins were all business. There was none of the usual banter and social niceties that had marked the introductions of all of their other games.

"Hi, I'm Lily and this is Drew," Lily said, extending her hand and flashing them her most charming, and, in Drew's opinion, her most irresistible, smile. "We're from Charlotte, although we don't go to the same…"

"We go first," the twin whose nametag identified him as Jonathon, interrupted Lily.

"Do you go by Jonathon or John?" Lily asked, undeterred. She was determined to make nice with their intimidating (*adj,* inducing a feeling of fear, awe, or inadequacy in somebody) opponents.

"Jonathon," Jonathon said, without cracking a smile.

"And I assume you go by Benjamin rather than Ben?" Drew asked the other twin, touching Lily's foot under the table.

Benjamin, a boy of even fewer words than his brother, simply nodded.

Lily pretended to busy herself with filling out their score sheet, but instead she wrote Drew a note, which she pushed over to him once she'd written it.

"No brain cells left for social skills," Drew read, trying hard not to laugh out loud.

He had never wanted to beat a team more.

The Mitchell twins picked their seven letters and then, while Drew and Lily were still picking theirs from the bag, laid down all seven letters.

"The blank is a U," Johnathon said, laying down the word TURKEYS. "Eighty-four."

"Nice start," Lily commented magnanimously (*adv,* very generously, kindly or forgivingly), although she might as well have been talking to the tile bag for all the acknowledgment or response she received.

Thanking his early morning review of short J words earlier that day, Drew suggested playing JAKE, with the J on the triple letter score, above the K in TURKEYS. It would yield 31 points and leave them with I E S and T, very bingo-friendly letters. Lily agreed.

The Mitchell twins, after a quick and whispered consultation behind their clipboard, announced that they were exchanging three tiles.

Drew and Lily had picked another T, along with an R and a U.

"We can do RUSTIEST off the S," Drew said, beginning to take the tiles from their rack. Lily placed her hand on his arm to stop him.

"How about TRUSTIES?" she asked. "They may not know that word."

"Yeah, but isn't that double e?" Drew whispered back. "I don't think it's spelled that way."

"It is," Lily replied. "I know because I thought the same thing and challenged Jeremy once. It might draw the challenge."

"If you're sure," Drew said, nervously agreeing. He placed the tiles on the board and tallied the points. "Sixty," he announced.

The Mitchell twins looked at each other and then both said, in unison, "Challenge."

"I sure hope she's right about this one," Drew thought as he nervously headed over to the computer with Benjamin.

Green screen. The play is acceptable.

Back at the table, no words were exchanged. One look at their returning partners' faces, one registering dismay and the other joy, signaled what the outcome of the challenge had been to those who had remained at the table.

Drew and Lily drew another T, which they hooked on the end of TRUSTIES to form the words TRUSTIEST and AVERT for another 36 points.

The Mithcell twins responded with another blank and another bingo. They played DUCTILE (*adj,* able to be drawn out into wire or hammered in very thin sheets), with the D below the triple word square and hooking the E on top of the T in TURKEYS, for 65 points.

The score was 149 to 127.

Drew's and Lily's rack looked ugly and unmanageable. It certainly didn't seem conducive (*adj ,* tending to encourage or bring about a good or intended result) to making a bingo. The seven tiles they had picked, and put on their rack in this order, were G P C I O N L.

Lily saw that they had an ING suffix so she put those letters together at the end of their rack. That left P C O and L.

"Too bad there's no open P on the board," Drew thought. "We could do clopping."

"How about COUP?" Lily asked pointing to the U in DUCTILE, "Just to get rid of the C and the P?"

"Hold on," Drew said, unwilling to abandon playing an ING bingo that turn just yet. He looked at all the open tiles on the board. And then it hit him.

"Policing!" he whispered to Lily, although his whisper was practically a yell thanks to the adrenaline (*n,* a hormone secreted in the adrenal gland that raises blood pressure, produces a rapid heartbeat, and acts as a neurotransmitter when the body is subjected to stress or danger) and excitement he felt in spotting a bingo, on a double double no less.

"You rock!" Lily said, clapping her hands.

Drew added up the points, then multiplied them by four since the P was on a double word square and the G was as well. He then added fifty points and had trouble keeping the "Ha! Take that!" out of his voice as he announced, "One hundred and two."

Drew and Lily were now ahead 229 to 149, despite the fact that their opponents had bingoed twice in a row and used both of the blanks.

The Mithcells, clearly feeling defeated, and making it abundantly clear they were not accustomed to feeling that way, played ADOBO for 18 points.

Next to the second O in ADOBO was a triple letter square. And five squares below that was a double word square.

Both Drew and Lily knew, without even having to discuss it with each other, that they wanted to place their F in the triple letter square and create a word going down so that the F's four points would be tripled twice. Moving the letters around on their rack, their hands overlapping as they came up with the same word simultaneously, they looked at each other and nodded, grinning. They played FAMISH for 57 points.

"Two hundred eighty six," Benjamin Mithcell mumbled dejectedly, adding the 57 points to their score. Drew and Lily had a lead of over 100 points.

The Mitchells made some other good plays, including one more bingo (DETAILING through the T and the I that were already on the board) but Drew and Lily never gave up their lead, winning the game 475 to 405.

"Great game," Lily gushed, extending her hand.

"You got everything," Jonathon spit out, while his brother furiously wiped his eyes, in a futile effort to fight back the tears that were lining their rims.

Drew felt bad for them. They were the odds-on favorites and they were just beaten by tournament newbies. And they didn't even get as far as they had last year. He could understand how devastated they were. Sore losers he could handle. But being rude to Lily? Not okay.

"Uh, let's see," Drew said, pretending to study his score sheet, where Lily had meticulously recorded each play and tracked all the tiles that had been played. "You got both blanks, the K, the Q and two of the S's." He looked up from the score sheet to stare directly at Jonathon. "So how exactly does that translate into our getting everything?"

Jonathon's response was to sign the result slip, gather up his papers, and follow his brother out of the room, all without saying another word.

Lily still stood there, her hand outstretched.

"Oh, we enjoyed it too." She said, shaking an imaginary opponent's hand. "Thanks so much for taking the loss so well and being such good sports."

Drew hugged her.

"We beat the odious Mitchell twins," he said. "We are what I like to call the conquerors of all slimy opponents."

"We are," Lily said, squeezing him back, "what I like to call one heck of a great team."

CHAPTER EIGHTEEN

"This is Hannah," Lucy said, pulling a red-headed girl whose face appeared to have an explosion of freckles and whose shirt proclaimed she was from Bend, Oregon, over to where Drew and Lily were sitting with Elliott Springer and most of the other Randolph kids. "I met her last night at the ice cream social."

"Hi," Hannah said, grinning. "Congrats on making it to the finals. That's awesome."

"Thanks," Drew and Lily said in unison. They couldn't quite believe it themselves. Neither could Elliott. In fact, he kept saying just that, shaking his head with the sheer wonder of it all. "I knew you'd do well, but top two. Wow. I can't believe it."

"So are you guys ready?" Lucy asked them.

"Yeah, as ready as we're going to be," Drew said, wishing he could have a little more time to cram. Lily's arrival that morning, as welcome as it had been, had cut short his study session. He'd never gotten to the Q without U words or the good vowel dumps, like AIOLI (*n,* mayonnaise flavored with garlic, used especially to garnish fish and vegetables) and COOEE (*v,* to cry out shrilly).

"We're just waiting for them to come and get us for the special room we play in," Lily explained.

"We're all going to get to watch them on a big TV screen," Mr. Springer explained. "And ESPN will be in there filming the game too." He shook his head again. "It's just unbelievable."

"No," Lucy said, interrupting Mr. Springer's litanies of how unbelievable it was. "I mean, are you ready for Hannah's poem?"

"Hannah's what?" Lily asked, not wanting to be rude but really, she just wanted to chill with Drew and it didn't seem like the most opportune moment to meet someone new and hear her recite some poetry.

"My SCRABBLE good luck poem," Hannah explained. "I wrote it last night during the ice cream social and Lucy really liked it."

"It's awesome," Lucy gushed. "Brandon and I lost all our games this morning but then I had Hannah do her poem for us…"

"With the tile rack blessing," Hannah interrupted. "Don't forget the all-important tile rack blessing,"

"Right," Lucy agreed, grinning "Anyway, we won our next game *big*, so it totally works."

"Okay," Lily said, putting her arm through Drew's and turning them both to face freckle-faced Hannah. "Go for it. We'll take any help we can get."

Drew had had more physical contact with a girl in the span of two days than he'd had in his entire life up until that point. At first he thought everyone could see his entire body react to Lily's touch, whether it was squeezing his hand or putting her arm around him or even jokingly hitting him, but no one seemed to be snickering or running outside to see if pigs were flying. And the more she did it, casually linking an arm through his or putting her hand on his shoulder as she leaned over to whisper something to him, the more natural and right it felt. It was still thrilling, and his pulse still sped up to an alarming rate, but it was more pleasurable than scary, and Drew now knew without a shadow of a doubt that his mom had serious I told you so rights. There was no debating whether or not you liked someone. It was not something you had to question or analyze or talk yourself into. When it hits, your brain is not the only organ telling you; other organs send up all sorts of flares as well. No doubt about it, Mara Founts-Hiltone was right. Pit a pat! Pit a pat!

Hannah, oblivious to the pit a pat symphony going on inside Drew, took the wooden tile rack she was holding and touched both Drew and Lily on their shoulders as she recited, in a voice reminiscent (*adj*, suggesting similarities or comparisons with something or somebody else) of a chant,

Oh mighty Tile God, Oh Mighty Tile God
May good letters come to me.
Oh mighty Tile God, Oh Mighty Tile God
Give me the X, the J, the Q plus the Z.
I know that you need skill to win,
Which I must have all on my own
But think of me up there in the sky
When you're on your giant SCRABBLE throne.
Oh mighty Tile God, oh mighty Tile God

S's and blanks are grand
Oh mighty Tile God, oh mighty Tile God
My game lies in your hand.

When Hannah was done, everyone clapped and cheered.

The Mitchell twins, who happened to be walking by right at that moment, shook their heads in disgust.

"They haven't won yet," Benjamin said, rolling his eyes.

"Yeah, and they're not even that good." Jonathon muttered. "They're just lucky."

Drew overheard them, and he was tempted to chase after them and set the record straight yet again. He wanted to tell them, *again,* that they'd beaten them fair and square. That he and Lily had a lot more than luck on their side. That they had *won;* the Mitchells had *lost,* and they should just deal with it. But he realized – and Dr. Anderson later spent a lot of time belaboring this moment, because he said it was an important epiphany (*n,* a sudden intuitive leap of understanding, especially through an ordinary but striking occurrence) – that they weren't worth it. Instead, he turned to Hannah and praised her poetic prowess (*n,* exceptional ability or skill).

"Great poem," he said, giving Hannah a big thumbs up. "If we win, you get a percentage of our winnings."

"Hey, speak for yourself," Lily interjected. "I've got big plans for those $5000!"

"Yeah, like taking your coach out for a lobster dinner, right?" Mr. Springer joked.

"How about buying you a big box of Kleenex instead?" Mohammed suggested. They were all having fun teasing Mr. Springer because he was practically in tears about how proud he was of all of them. "I thought it would be great if you'd each won a game," their coach told them, when they'd all gathered around after the final game, "but you all exceeded my expectations. I really couldn't be prouder."

"Well duh, you've got a team competing in the finals," Brandon said.

Mr. Springer was quick to correct him. "But that's not what makes me proud," he pointed out.

Lily opened her mouth in astonishment, but she also winked at Elliott to communicate that no offense was taken. She knew him well enough to know that he would have been proud of her – and the rest of the team – no matter how they'd placed. And as thrilled as he was with her and Drew's performance – and the fact that they were now vying for the top prize – she knew that he was just as pleased with Cecelia's coming out of her shell a bit and David's vastly improved vocabulary and the fact that Marcus had picked the SCRABBLE tournament over a basketball game. And with four games in the win column, Jennifer and Cecelia had placed in the top twenty, while Brandon and Lucy's game against the team from Cambridge, Massachusetts that Drew and Lily would be facing in the final match, in which they'd bingoed twice and fought a valiant (*adj, characterized by or performed with bravery but often ending in failure*) fight but lost nonetheless, with a score of 416, had earned them the prize for highest loss.

"Okay, we're ready for you," Jane Ratsey Williams, who was in charge of the School SCRABBLE Tournament, said as she approached their little group. "I can only take Drew and Lily back to the room, but the rest of you will be able to sit up front in the screening room to watch the game as it progresses on a big screen."

"Cool," David said.

"Will there be popcorn?" Marcus asked in jest (*n, something done or said in a playful, joking manner*).

"Yes, there will be popcorn and drinks and another special treat," Mrs. Williams said, "plus Joe Shoeman will serve as commentator for the game."

"Man, you guys sure know how to put on a tournament," Mohammed gushed.

Mrs. Williams flashed him a big smile. Lily had insisted all weekend that Jane Ratsey Williams looked just like Meryl Streep, something Drew didn't really appreciate until that moment. But when she smiled, motioning for Drew and Lily to follow her, he could totally see it. And it made sense. Why shouldn't this perfect weekend and tournament, during which Drew had not once felt like the lowest of the low, and had even, at times, felt downright normal, powerful even, why shouldn't it culminate with a movie star leading them off to their final moment of glory?

The Cambridge team was already in the room, being interviewed by the ESPN reporter. They were both 8th graders and both girls, and they were explaining to the reporter that this was their third time playing together at the National School SCRABBLE Championship and that they had finished in the top ten last year. Drew and Lily had already met them during the semi-final game, when all four teams vying for the top two spots had played apart from the rest of the school teams, and they seemed nice. And smart. Brandon and Lucy had already warned them about *that*. "Minusha, that's the Indian girl," Brandon reported back, stating the obvious, "both her parents are doctors, so she knows all these weird medical terms. I wouldn't challenge them if I were you, even if the word looks like it couldn't possibly be a word." And Lucy added that Danielle, the other girl, was plenty intimidating in her own right. "She plays super quickly," she said. "So you feel crunched for time because you never have time to think during their turns since they make their moves before you've even replaced the tiles you've just played."

Both Minusha and Danielle waved at Drew and Lily, grinning.

"Welcome to the circus," Minusha said.

"Your turn," Danielle said, gesturing towards the camera.

The two girls stepped away and made room for Drew and Lily under the bright lights. The ESPN reporter, who acted as if covering a kids' SCRABBLE tournament was akin to covering the Super Bowl, greeted them and positioned them in front of the big camera. "Just talk to the camera," he advised. "And try to ignore all of this," he motioned to all of the equipment, the bright lights, the hustle and bustle all around them as the board was set up and the tiles were counted, and the murmurs of excitement as the other 102 teams and their parents and coaches entered the adjoining room and got settled in their seats.

"So how long have you two been playing SCRABBLE?" the reporter asked.

Drew and Lily looked at each other.

"Together?" Drew asked.

"Less than a month," Lily replied, laughing.

"But it feels like much longer than that," Drew stopped himself from adding.

"And what first attracted you each to the game?"

Lily explained about her weekly games with Jeremy, which the reporter found fascinating. He asked her lots of follow up questions, during which Drew let his mind wander. He couldn't quite believe he was standing here, being interviewed on ESPN, standing next to a beautiful girl, and no one was protesting that there was something wrong with this picture. That something didn't fit. That he didn't belong.

"So anything you'd like to say to Aidan, back there in a cast in Charlotte, North Carolina?" the reporter asked, and Drew realized with alarm that he was talking to *him*.

"Um, I wish you could be here," (Drew hoped the "Not!" thought bubble above his head didn't translate onto the TV screen) "and we'll do our best to bring you home the trophy."

The reporter then asked them for some more information off-camera, that he would use to fill in the piece later, and then it was time to take their seats. When they did, and it was time to start, Drew could hear a muffled cheer from the viewing room. David told him later that the remaining teams and their parents and coaches had each been given chocolate bars with the SCRABBLE logo on them so they were all sugared-up and pumped for the action to start. Plus Joe Shoeman had entertained the crowd while they were waiting with stories of some of his best games and SCRABBLE moments, like when he'd scored 732 on a game in Singapore during the World SCRABBLE Championship or when he'd scored 293 on a single out play, putting down the word SQUEEZER on the triple triple.

"It was so cool *during* the game too," Jennifer added, "because he would tell us before you guys moved what he thought was the best move."

"And he'd tell us when he thought you guys came up with something good or if he thought there was something else you should have done." Marcus added.

"Yes, I took notes," Cecelia remarked. "I can copy them for you if you'd like. It was very informative."

"He was pretty sure you guys had it won towards the end," Brandon said.

"Yeah, he said the only way they could win it, since most of the power tiles had been played by then, was for Manusha and Danielle to bingo."

Drew had felt pretty confident then too. Drew and Lily had 426 points to Manusha and Danielle's 338. The only way Manusha and Danielle could win was to bingo, but there were very few open bingo lanes. They did have a blank – Drew and Lily knew exactly what their opponents had on their final rack thanks to Lily's tile tracking – but otherwise their letters were not particularly bingo-friendly, especially since there were no S hooks on the board. They would have to bingo across through the D in SUDDEN or start on the triple word square in the upper left corner and end in R. Their only other option was to do something starting with the U in JAUP (*v,* to splash), since Drew and Lily had blocked the S hook by playing OX above the P in JAUP on the triple word square.

Manusha and Danielle had F, N, S, E, L, A and a blank on their rack. They also had a whopping 14 minutes left on their clock. As they struggled to find a bingo, knowing as well as everyone else that it was the only way they could win, the minutes ticked away. With each minute that elapsed, Drew and Lily felt more and more assured of their victory. They had written down their opponents' tiles on their own score sheet and had tried coming up with possible bingos using Manusha and Danielle's tiles, but they couldn't find one. They tried putting the N under the U in JAUP and starting a word with the UN prefix, but all they could come up with was UNFALSER, and they didn't think that was good. If Manusha and Danielle played that, Drew and Lily would challenge and they'd head to Zyzzyva liking their odds.

But that is not what the girls played. With two minutes remaining, Manusha turned to Danielle and whispered furiously in her ear. Danielle's response was to turn and plant a big smooch on Manusha's cheek. Together, they placed their F *above* the U in JAUP, to form the word FOX and begin their bingo with FU. Drew and Lily watched helplessly as their opponents proceeded to place the N, then the E, then the blank (which they said was an R) then the A then the L and then the S.

"Eighty six points," they said in unison, after spelling out FUNERALS. They then hit the stop button on the clock, since that was their final turn. "And out."

Drew and Lily scrambled to crunch the numbers. Eighty-six points gave Manusha and Danielle 424 points to Drew and Lily's 426 points. But that was without factoring in the points on their rack. Even if everything they'd been left with was a one-point tile, which it wasn't, they still would have lost. As it was, the W, G,I, E, E, L and O on their rack gave Manusha and Danielle critical points.

And the win.

They found out later, when they dissected the game in private and shared what they'd each been thinking, away from all the hoopla (*n,* noisy, excited commotion or joyous celebrating) and craziness of the awards ceremony and the throngs of well-wishers and the cameras, that they'd each felt like the trophy had been in their hands and then yanked away from them. They had each been convinced, in the way you just know something to be true, like that your mom will always love you, no matter how badly you screw up, that they'd already won the game. So processing the final bingo, and the fact that it meant the game was over and that they had not, in fact, won it, that they had *lost* it by 20 points, well, that was a lot to take in, especially when the ESPN camera was zoomed in on your faces.

Drew was the first to stick out his hand, followed immediately by Lily.

"Congrats," he said. "That was an unbelievable find."

"We thought we had you," Lily added. "We didn't think there was a bingo there."

"Neither did we!" Danielle said, her voice bubbling over with excitement.

"Thank God we had enough time to find it," Manusha added.

John Williams walked over to the table and congratulated all of them.

"What an exciting game," he remarked, his eyes sparkling behind his black-rimmed glasses. "You all should be very proud of yourselves."

Drew knew it was just a social nicety, something you say to make the losers feel better, but for some reason it rang true. He *was* proud of himself. He and Lily had enjoyed a phenomenal run. And they had nothing to be ashamed of.

Mr. Springer rounded the corner and engulfed them both in a huge bear hug. This time he really was crying. "Wow," he said. "Wow."

"For someone who coaches a SCRABBLE club," Lily said, laughing, "you sure are a man of few words."

"Yeah, you might want to think about expanding your vocabulary a bit," Drew teased, smiling.

John Williams took the stage and introduced the head of Hasbro, the company that sponsored the tournament and markets and sells the game of SCRABBLE, "that game we all know is so much more than a game." He presented a huge, oversized check for $5000 to Danielle and Manusha and then a similarly cartoonish check for $2000 to the second place winners. Drew and Lily took the stage amidst huge cheers. They could see Mr. Springer and David and Mohammed and Brandon and Lucy and Marcus and Irwin and Cecelia and Jennifer whooping and hollering and high-fiving each other. Drew made up his mind right there and then that part of his share of the winnings would go to a big SCRABBLE club celebration when they got back to Charlotte. Although they'd need to do it some night or weekend when Lily could come too. Because it wouldn't be right without her.

CHAPTER NINETEEN

"The best part," Drew told Dr. Anderson, knowing he'd appreciate Drew's candor (that was, after all, what he was supposed to do during these sessions; lay bare his soul and his innermost thoughts, even if they didn't necessarily reflect well on him), "was seeing Matt Santoni's face."

"Tell me more," Dr. Anderson said, the twinkle in his eyes defying his neutral expression. "What did Matt's face look like?"

"Well, it's not like I punched him or anything," Drew explained, trying to put into words exactly what had been so satisfying about the day, "but, well, it was as close as I'm ever going to come to fighting back."

Dr. Anderson nodded, his cue for Drew to continue.

"I mean, I was standing up there, on stage, and so I was, you know, above him. That, alone, made him look so much smaller and not nearly as menacing as he is when we're face to face. And everyone – and I mean *everyone*, the entire school! – was cheering for *me*. And for Lily and Aidan, of course, and the rest of our team."

Drew's face flushed thinking back on that moment, just as it had every time since the pep rally that he'd relived in his mind, which was more times than he was willing to admit, even to Dr. Anderson. Mrs. Villroy had greeted the returning SCRABBLE Club with the kind of fanfare usually reserved for the football team, and the school-wide pep rally was only part of the hoopla. They had been featured on the Raider Report, the weekly school-wide TV show, and she had created a premier spot in the front hallway's display case for their trophy. What turned the tide, however, and made students who would ordinarily have mocked the triumphs of a lowly SCRABBLE Club cheer with abandon at the pep rally, was the flyer she sent home to every single student's family extolling (*v*, to praise somebody or something with great enthusiasm and admiration) the accomplishments of the entire team and heaping particular praise on Drew and Lily's 2nd place finish. The clincher was the date and time of the ESPN airing, on which Drew and Lily would be featured. Most RMS students, especially those who gave Drew the most grief, didn't know or care about the National School SCRABBLE Championship. But ESPN, *that* was speaking their language. ESPN they knew. And the fact that Drew was going to *be* on ESPN, that he was going to have over 30 minutes of air time, sandwiched between the professional athletes and sportscasters these kids revered, well, that immediately and inexplicably catapulted Drew from nerd to, if not superstar, then, at a minimum, a kid who no longer deserved to be taunted or mocked.

Everyone got the memo but Matt Santoni. So ingrained was his bullying instinct, and so established was his pattern of interacting with Drew, that the excitement about Drew and the turnaround of his status in the school seemed to infuriate Matt to an all-new level of contempt (*n,* a powerful feeling of dislike toward somebody or something considered to be worthless, inferior, or undeserving of respect).

"Hey, gayboy," he hissed menacingly, when Drew was on his way to Latin class on the Wednesday after his triumphant return from Rhode Island. He moved to block Drew's path in the hallway, but his teammates, the very ones who had backed him up and joined in the Drew-bashing as recently as a week earlier, instead crowded around Drew to high five him and ask him if ESPN had given him any cool stuff to bring home. And when everyone stood up to give Drew and the rest of the SCRABBLE team a standing ovation at the pep rally, Matt, who was front and center (thanks to Mrs. Villroy's strategically placing the football team in the front row) was conspicuous in his refusal to get up. Drew watched with surprise and unabashed (*adj,* not ashamed or embarrassed by something) delight as Coach Harkins grabbed big, powerful Matt Santoni by his elbow and hoisted him out of his seat.

But the cherry on top of the Matt Santoni ice cream sundae came later, when the pep rally was over and everyone was filing out of the auditorium. Drew could hear snippets of conversation, and from the sound of it Mr. Springer was going to have to purchase a few more SCRABBLE boards to accommodate all of the newfound interest in the game. Drew was standing with Lily, introducing her to his teachers who made their way over to congratulate him and meet his partner, when Coach Harkins dragged Matt Santoni across the stage. Drew's heart began to race in that familiar and ingrained panic mode that Matt Santoni encounters always entailed.

"That's *him*," he whispered to Lily. "That's *Matt Santoni*."

Lily knew all about Matt Santoni. She knew all about the bullying, the gay slurs, the inferiority Drew felt because of his size and the fact that, with Aidan out of school, he had practically no one with whom to eat lunch. She knew how alone he felt at school, how socially inept (*adj,* lacking the confidence or skill for a particular task) he was in almost every situation involving kids his age, and how he'd become so despondent and angry that he'd been seeing a psychiatrist. In fact, Lily knew more about Drew's daily battles at Randolph and his fears and insecurities than Dr. Anderson had learned about him in almost a year of weekly therapy sessions.

Lily was not paid to hear about Drew's angst, nor was she professionally trained in how to assuage (*v,* to provide relief from something distressing or painful) it, but she had one huge advantage over Dr. Anderson, and anyone else for that matter. She saw what was good and noble and amazing about Drew – his incredible intellect; his maturity beyond his years; his endearing modesty and self-doubts; his self-deprecating humor; and his kind and gentle nature, so rare in a teenaged boy – and, through her, Drew began to believe that perhaps he wasn't the biggest loser in the universe. If someone as fabulous and beautiful and objectively way, way above him on the social hierarchy that defined all middle school interactions liked *him*, he couldn't be that bad.

And the fact that Lily liked him, in the pit a pat heart way the *he* liked *her*, was now firmly established. It was not something to fantasize about or wish for when throwing a penny into the fountain at SouthPark Mall or daydream about during Algebra II class or on the bus ride to school. It was real, and he knew it was real because she'd told him so when they'd gone over to Aidan's house together to show him the trophy and to give him the get well gifts the entire team had purchased for him in Providence.

As they were sitting on his front steps, waiting for Mara to come pick them up (Aidan had enjoyed the visit but needed rest after all the excitement and the opening of the gifts, so Drew and Lily had chosen to wait out in the sunshine rather than inside the house, where Aidan's mom was peppering them with questions), Drew turned to Lily and said thank you.

"What for?" she asked. She'd planned on getting him something to commemorate their great teamwork, but she hadn't done so yet.

Inexplicably, Drew felt a lump in his throat.

"For being so nice to me," he finally managed to say.

Lily turned to him.

"What is your problem?" she demanded to know. "Don't you get it? I like you. I *want* to spend time with you. You're, like, the coolest guy I know. And the smartest. My friends Samantha and Jessie have heard all about you…"

Drew just stared at her, dumbfounded by her reaction and torrent of words.

"And if you don't try to kiss me soon, *I'm* going to have to start seeing Dr. Anderson!"

The welcome mat was thrown at his feet. Drew couldn't help but walk across it.

He kissed her.

For once, Dr. Anderson didn't ask him how it made him feel. He knew.

"So, *that's* Matt Santoni," Lily said out loud, instinctively taking Drew's hand. "Looks like he's in trouble."

Sure enough, Coach Harkins pushed Matt forward.

"I'm sorry," Matt mumbled, staring at the stage floor.

"What for?" Coach Harkins prompted gruffly.

"For not acting respectfully during the pep rally," Matt said, spitting out each word because he had to.

His eye must have caught sight of Lily holding Drew's hand, because he looked up suddenly, startled. Without using any words, he was able to convey, with his look of disgust and surprise, "What's a girl like *that* doing with a loser like *you.*"

"That's okay," Drew said, eager to have the awkward and forced apology over.

"Yeah," Lily piped up, looking Matt Santoni directly in the eyes. "He'd have to care to notice, neither of which he did."

Matt just stared at her, dumbfounded.

"So, I'll see you tonight, Drew," Lily said, more for Matt's benefit than Drew's. She leaned forward to hug Drew, lingering long enough to whisper in his ear, "I'll take a nerd like you over a loser like that any day."

Drew grinned like an idiot while Matt just stared at him and the departing Lily, back and forth, like he was watching a tennis match.

Drew knew Matt would continue to try to torment him, but he suspected the days of calling him Gayboy were finally at an end.

CHAPTER TWENTY

Lily put the wreath of flowers in her hair and looked in the mirror. A girl in a long, flowing purple dress, the same purple as the irises circling her braided bun, stared back at her. With the loan of her mom's pearl necklace and earrings, Lily grudgingly admitted to herself that she looked pretty nice. She was still more tomboy than priss, and dressing up held little appeal to her, but when the occasion called for it, it was kind of fun to get all dolled up.

"Oh my gosh, you look stunning," Sally said, walking in behind her and hugging her from behind. "And," she added, a lump in her throat, "so grown up."

"Right back at you," Lily said, looking at her mom's reflection in the mirror.

"Thanks," Sally said, blushing. "Not bad for an old woman, eh?"

Sally had finally stopped nagging Lily about going out and acting like a teenager. Now that she'd gone to Drew's spring formal and he'd escorted her to the Crestdale dance, Lily's social life met with her mother's standards. Now it was Lily's turn to nag.

"You are *not* old, Mom," Lily said. "And besides, you always said you are only as old as you feel."

"Well, in that case," Sally giggled, "I feel about sixteen."

"I'm going to go help Jeremy get ready," Lily said, giving her mother a peck on the cheek.

"Oh, Drew's doing that," Sally replied. "He arrived while you were getting dressed. They came early because Mara is setting up the cake."

"Ooh, I want to see it," Lily exclaimed, running downstairs.

The cake was set up on the dining room table, high atop a platter that had hundreds of wooden SCRABBLE tiles strewn around its base as decoration. The cake itself was white, with oversized, marzipan

SCRABBLE tiles spelling out C ON G R A T U L A T I O N S across its top.

"Oh, that's magnificent," Lily exclaimed. "You've outdone yourself," she said to Mara, who walked in from the kitchen with an icing bag to add some last-minute touch ups to her creation.

"Thanks," Mara was pleased and relieved that the cake had survived the drive across town. "And don't you look beautiful."

"Yes, you sure do," Drew said, having left Jeremy in front of the computer and gone in search of Lily.

He told Dr. Anderson, in what they'd both agreed was his last session, that he had resolved to share more of his thought bubbles with Lily. "She had no idea I liked her," he marveled. "I thought it was so painfully obvious, but she swears she didn't know."

Dr. Anderson chuckled.

"When I asked my wife out," he confessed, "I had to ask her three or four times before she finally understood that I was asking her out on a date."

"But that's just the thing," Drew said. "I actuallyhave such an easy time talking to Lily. I'm not my usual loser self."

"Hmmm" Dr. Anderson said. "I see."

Drew was actually going to miss Dr. Anderson's *Hmmms* and *I sees*.

"Could it be that perhaps that's because Lily doesn't see you that way?" Dr. Anderson asked.

And that was the most wonderful and miraculous thing of all. Not only did Lily not see him as a loser, she saw him as someone wonderful. Someone she wanted to hang out with. Someone she wanted to take her to her school dance and someone she liked more than a SCRABBLE partner. Drew could still conjure up that delicious surprise he'd felt on Aidan's front steps when he'd discovered that Lily felt the same way about him that he did about her.

Drew took Lily's hand and led her out of the dining room. He had something he wanted to give her and he did not need his mother standing there, beaming at them as if they were a cute new litter of puppies.

"I have something for you," he said, giving Lily a small box wrapped in a big purple bow.

Lily's eyes lit up. "A present?" she asked. "I love presents! I would have gotten myself a boyfriend a long time ago if I'd known it involved spontaneous gift giving."

Drew smiled back at her. Much like the ESPN cameras and the thrills of the School SCRABBLE Touranment had seemed unreal and the stuff of fantasies, so did the idea of his being anyone's boyfriend. And Lily's, no less.

Lily untied the ribbon and opened up the box. Inside was a silver chain with four silver SCRABBLE tiles dangling from it, spelling out L I L Y.

"I thought you could wear it to tournaments," Drew explained, "to bring you luck."

"Won't I have *you* there with me?" Lily asked, her eyes twinkling. She reached over and kissed him on the cheek. "Thank you. I *love* it."

Drew helped her put it on, and then continued holding her hand as they headed over to the backyard to see what they could do to help. The chairs were already set up and decorated with ribbons and many of the guests were already milling around talking to one another or had taken their seats. Drew and Lily ran up to Cecelia and Jennifer and hugged them. They hadn't seen them all summer so there was a lot of catching up to do.

They both told Drew how weird it was going to be to have SCRABBLE Club at Randolph without him. They said he'd be missed. Never in a million years would Drew have believed that his presence would be missed at that school. "Just my luck," he thought to himself, "that I finally fit in with some kids now that I'm gone!"

Drew saw Mr. Springer (who told him it was now okay to call him Elliott since Drew was no longer a Randolph student but Drew just couldn't quite bring himself to do it) and he walked over to say hello. Elliott Springer was wearing a grey suit and purple tie, and his customary sneakers had been replaced with shiny black shoes.

"Man, you clean up nice," Drew said. "I hardly recognized you."

"You're looking pretty dapper yourself," Elliott said, smiling at Drew, who had probably only grown a couple of inches since the beginning of 8th grade but who looked and acted a foot taller than the insecure brainiac he had taught for the last three years.

"Talking about transformations," Drew commented, "wait until you see Jeremy!"

As if on cue, Jeremy emerged from the house and surveyed his unfamiliar backyard. He looked bewildered (*adj,* extremely confused) and flustered, but then his face lit up when he saw Drew and Elliott standing together.

"Drew! Elliott!" he cried out, so loudly that almost everyone turned around.

Both Drew and Elliott were familiar to Jeremy, and seeing them both, together, added a welcome and comforting touch to what was striking Jeremy as not how things should be. There were all sorts of people in his yard, he was not allowed to wear his Homer Simpson slippers, and there were way too many chairs. Only the patio chairs belonged in the backyard, not all of these extra chairs with ribbons on them.

"Hey Jer, you sure look spiffy," Elliott said, being careful not to hug him.

"Are you ready to come sit with me?" Drew asked. Lily had caught his eye and motioned that it was time before disappearing into the house to help her Mom.

"I'll sit with you, Drew," Jeremy said. "But there are too many people and too many chairs."

"Don't worry, Jeremy," Drew said. "You only need to hang out here a little bit and then you get to go back in for Jeopardy. And none of these people will interfere with that. They all know you have to watch Jeopardy at 7:00 pm. Promise."

Jeremy nodded. "I like Jeopardy," he said. "I watch it every night."

"I know that," Drew said, winking at Elliott. Anyone who had spent any time at all with this family knew that.

Drew and Jeremy sat down in the front row of chairs and everyone who had not yet found a seat did. Drew turned back to see where his parents had ended up and he saw a slew of familiar faces. Mrs. Villroy was sitting with several Randolph teachers, and Lily's good friends Samantha and Jessie were there with their families. He also saw Malcom and David, who looked extremely uncomfortable in button down shirts and ties, and Lily's Aunt Nicole and her family. He saw his mom, who blew him a kiss, and his dad, who smiled and put his arm around his mom.

Ginger Fung, Randolph's music teacher, was seated directly in front of Drew with the enormous cello Drew had helped her bring to that spot. After looking at her watch, she sat upright, took a deep breath, and began to play. Drew had warned Jeremy about the music and he had talked him through everything that was going to happen, but still he felt Jeremy tense and begin to fidget nervously.

"It's okay, Jer," Drew whispered to him. "Remember? We talked about this. Elliott is going to walk up here any minute."

"And then Lily. And then my mom." Jeremy said. "Elliott. Then Lily. Then my mom. Elliott. Then Lily. Then my mom."

Drew fervently (*adv,* marked with fervor) hoped that things would happen as planned. He didn't want to be made out to be a liar. Jeremy would never forgive him.

Elliott walked in when Mrs. Fung's cello was joined by a flute, and he strode to the front and then turned to face everyone. He winked at Drew and Jeremy. They had all agreed it would be easier for Jeremy to sit with Drew and face Elliott and his mom and sister than to stand up with them and face everyone else. They had tried to think of everything they could to make this easier on Jeremy but still include him in the festivities.

Next Lily walked in and Drew's heart swelled at the sight of her.

"LILY LOOKS PRETTY!" Jeremy said, loud enough for almost everyone to hear.

Lily blushed as everyone laughed and murmured their concurrence.

"She sure does," Drew whispered to Jeremy. And then, without knowing why or thinking it through, he added, "I *really l*ike Lily."

"ME TOO," Jeremy said. "I REALLY LIKE LILY TOO."

Again, loud enough for everyone to hear.

This time Lily joined in the laughter and it was Drew's turn to blush.

When Sally walked in, both Lily and Elliott wiped tears from their eyes.

Drew and Lily knew Elliott was going to cry. They'd placed bets on how long it would take. Drew thought he'd at least make it to the I do's, but Lily predicted he'd be bawling when he saw her mom walking towards him.

"I won," Lily mouthed to Drew, grinning.

Drew grinned right back at her.

The prize for their bet was an entire day spent as the winner chose. It could include playing SCRABBLE, going to the movies, going out to eat, or taking a picnic to Freedom Park and feeding the ducks. It didn't really matter. What mattered is that, win or lose, the day would be spent with Lily. Drew felt exactly as he had when they'd lost the championship game at the National School SCRABBLE Tournament.

He was already a winner.

LaVergne, TN USA
28 June 2010

187669LV00005BA/198/P